The Angel Babies
Realm VI

The Angel Babies

Realm VI

Clive Alando Taylor

authorHOUSE

AuthorHouse™ UK
1663 Liberty Drive
Bloomington, IN 47403 USA
www.authorhouse.co.uk
Phone: 0800.197.4150

Published by AuthorHouse 08/11/2015

ISBN: 978-1-5049-8869-8 (sc)
ISBN: 978-1-5049-8870-4 (e)

Angelus Domini

Realm VI

INSPIRIT*ASPIRE*ESPRIT*INSPIRE*

Because of the things that have first become proclaimed within the spirit, and then translated in the soul, in order for the body to then become alive and responsive or to aspire, or to be inspired, if only then for the body to become a vessel, or a catalyst, or indeed an instrument of will, with which first the living spirit that gave life to it, along with the merits and the meaning of life, and the instruction and the interpretation of life, is simply to understand that the relationship between the spirit and the soul, are also the one living embodiment with which all things are one, and become connected and interwoven by creating, or causing what we can come to call, or refer to as the essence, or the cradle, or the fabric of life, which is in itself part physical and part spirit.

And so it is, that we are all brought in being, along with this primordial and spiritual birth, and along with this the presence or the origins of the spirit, which is also the fabric and the nurturer of the soul with which the body can be formed, albeit that by human standards, this act of nature however natural, can now take place through the act of procreation or consummation, and so it is with regard to this living spirit that we are also upon our natural and physical birth, given a name and a number, inasmuch that we represent, or become identified by a color, or upon our created formation and distinction of identity, we become recognized by our individuality.

1

Clive Alando Taylor

But concerning the Angels, it has always been of an interest to me how their very conception, or existence, or origin from nature and imagination, could have become formed and brought into being, as overtime I have heard several stories of how with the event of the first creation of man, that upon this event, that all the Angels were made to accept and to serve in God's creation of man, and that man was permitted to give command to these Angels in the event of his life, and the trials of his life which were to be mastered, but within this godly decree and narrative, we also see that there was all but one Angel that either disagreed or disapproved with, not only the creation of man, but also with the formation of this covenant between God and man, and that all but one Angel was Satan, who was somewhat displeased with God's creation of man, and in by doing so would not succumb or show respect or demonstrate servility or humility toward man or mankind.

As overtime it was also revealed to me, that with the creation of the Angels, that it was also much to their advantage as it was to ours, for the Angels themselves to adhere to this role and to serve in the best interest of man's endeavors upon the face of the earth, as long as man himself could demonstrate and become of a will and a nature to practice his faith with a spirit, and a soul, and a body that would become attuned to a godly or godlike nature, and in by doing so, and in by believing so, that all of his needs would be met with accordingly.

And so this perspective brings me to question my own faith and ideas about the concept and the ideology of Angels, insomuch so that I needed to address and to explore my own minds revelation, and to investigate that which I was told or at least that which I thought I knew concerning the Angels along with the juxtaposition that if Satan along with those Angels opposed to serving God's creation of man, and of those that did indeed seek to serve and to favor God's creation and to meet with the merits, and the dreams, and the aspirations of man, that could indeed cause us all to be at the mercy and the subjection of an externally influential and internal spiritual struggle or spiritual warfare, not only with ourselves, but also with our primordial and spiritual identity.

And also because of our own conceptual reasoning and comprehension beyond this event, is that we almost find ourselves astonished into believing that this idea of rights over our mortal souls or being, must have begun or started long ago, or at least long before any of us were even souls inhabiting our physical bodies here as a living presence upon the face of the earth, and such is this constructed dilemma behind our beliefs or identities, or the fact that the names, or the numbers that we have all been given, or that have at least become assigned to us, is simply because of the fact that we have all been born into the physical world.

As even I in my attempts, to try to come to terms with the very idea of how nature and creation could allow so many of us to question this reason of totality, if only for me to present to you the story of the Angel Babies, if only to understand, or to restore if your faith along with mine, back into the realms of mankind and humanity, as I have also come to reflect in my own approach and understanding of this narrative between God and Satan and the Angels, that also in recognizing that they all have the power to influence and to subject us to, as well as to direct mankind and humanity, either to our best or worst possibilities, if only then to challenge our primordial spiritual origin within the confines of our own lifestyles, and practices and beliefs, as if in our own efforts and practices that we are all each and every one of us, in subjection or at least examples and products of both good and bad influences.

Which is also why that in our spiritual nature, that we often call out to these heavenly and external Angelic forces to approach us, and to heal us, and to bless us spiritually, which is, or has to be made to become a necessity, especially when there is a humane need for us to call out for the assistance, and the welfare, and the benefit of our own souls, and our own bodies to be aided or administered too, or indeed for the proper gifts to be bestowed upon us, to empower us in such a way, that we can receive guidance and make affirmations through the proper will and conduct of a satisfactory lesson learnt albeit through this practical application and understanding, if only to attain spiritual and fruitful lives.

As it is simply by recognizing that we are, or at some point or another in our lives, have always somewhat been open, or subject to the interpretations of spiritual warfare by reason of definition, in that Satan's interpretation of creation is something somewhat of contempt, in that God should do away with, or even destroy creation, but as much as Satan can only prove to tempt, or to provoke God into this reckoning, it is only simply by inadvertently influencing the concepts, or the ideologies of man, that of which whom God has also created to be creators, that man through his trials of life could also be deemed to be seen in Satan's view, that somehow God had failed in this act of creation, and that Satan who is also just an Angel, could somehow convince God of ending creation, as Satan himself cannot, nor does not possess the power to stop or to end creation, which of course is only in the hands of the creator.

And so this brings me back to the Angels, and of those that are in favor of either serving, or saving mankind from his own end and destruction, albeit that we are caught up in a primordial spiritual fight, that we are all engaged in, or by reason of definition born into, and so it is only by our choices that we ultimately pay for our sacrifice, or believe in our rights to life, inasmuch that we are all lifted up to our greatest effort or design, if we can learn to demonstrate and to accept our humanity in a way that regards and reflects our greater desire or need, to be something more than what we choose to believe is only in the hands of God the creator or indeed a spirit in the sky.

It was very much my intention not to state the name of any particular place in the script as I thought that the telling of the story of the Angel Babies is in itself about believing in who you are, and also about facing up to your fears. The Angel Babies is also set loosely in accordance with the foretelling of the Bibles Revelations.

I thought it would be best to take this approach, as the writing of the script is also about the Who, What, Where, When, How and Why scenario that we all often deal with in our ongoing existence. It would also not be fair to myself or to anyone else who has read the Angel Babies to not acknowledge this line of questioning, for instance, who are we? What are we doing here? Where did we come from? And when will our true purpose be known? And how do we fulfil our true potential to better ourselves and others, the point of which are the statements that I am also making in the Angel Babies and about Angels in particular,

Is that if we reach far into our minds we still wonder Where did the Angels come from and what is their place in this world. I know sometimes that we all wish and pray for the miracle of life to reveal itself but the answer to this mystery truly lives within us and around us, I only hope that you will find the Angel Babies an interesting narrative and exciting story as I have had in bringing it to life, after all there could be an Angel Baby being born right now.

After these things I looked and behold a door standing open in Heaven and the first voice which I heard was like a (Trumpet!) speaking with me saying come up here and I will show you things which must take place after this. Immediately I was in the spirit and behold a throne set in Heaven and one sat on the throne and he who sat there was like a Jasper and a Sardius Stone in appearance, And there was a Rainbow around, In appearance like an Emerald.

Time is neither here or there, it is a time in between time as it is the beginning and yet the end of time. This is a story of the Alpha and the Omega, the first and the last and yet as we enter into this revelation, we begin to witness the birth of the Angel Babies a time of heavenly conception when dying Angels gave birth to Angelic children who were born to represent the order of the new world. The names of these Angel Babies remained unknown but they carried the Seal of their fathers written on their foreheads, and in all it totalled one hundred and forty four thousand Angels and this is the story of one of them.

It seemed to me that life was changing at an instant, and that the meaning of life itself had taken on another reality or interpretation of perception, and in my immediate awakening and thoughts of awareness, I now sensed that the physical world was now somewhat in decline Mankind's existence however unexpected and unpredictable in its desire and destiny to change and adapt and evolve, was not so much evolving, but in its entirety, the mortality and the mortality of Humanity was somehow on a collision course, that I sensed and feared would inevitably lead to its own nightmarish demise and outcome, that I now suppose would lead me sadly and dispiritedly to say that not so much the planet itself, but that the body which makes up the physicality of the Human body, could no longer support or withstand to sustain itself in such a profound state of such a worldly crisis of polluted and congested organisms.

Insomuch that what had led to developments of the dependency of Man advances towards using up the Earth's natural resources to build and to create and to innovate and to excavate the environment with which need Humans needed to sustain themselves, had by now underestimated that time enough upon this fragile Planet, and that of the Planets natural ability to heal and to replenish and adjust itself to any kind of manipulations and harvesting or mining and excavating of any kind, would indeed jeopardize and firstly be caused whilst directing itself through and also into an unbalance to attempt to correct itself, and so the Planet itself was also in resign whilst rebalancing itself, if only to maintain and support the very simplest the designs of life forms in both above and beneath and within the Earth's ecology.

As such was the ecology and the diversity, of the many different types of species and animal and sea and plant life, then so to were the many alien aspects and effects of the technologies which overtime had threatened and poisoned the Planet, so much so, that nature itself was in rebellion to the onslaught of developing Humans across the Globe, and such was the fight for the functions of the Earth to bring and sustain life, that somehow the Human being had created an environment that as soon as life had become born and awakened, then surely enough it had also overexposed and detrimentally began to bring about a prematurely death without the ability of knowledge or experience of how Man could or should learn to know and how to live and how to survive in such a harsh and changing climate.

As such was Humankinds resolve and resilience in becoming less and less effective to defend and withstand against such climatic changes, which was by now becoming more demanding whilst posing a threat to his natural habitat and environment that it had by now even led some of us amongst the Angeldom of the Empyreans, to become more consciously aware in our own observations, and in by doing so, we were left to form our own opinions that could ultimately divide us within our own personal concerns between the Heavens and Earth, as to whether we should have to intervene in any way shape or form to save this World of humanity from an ultimately and untimely inevitable fate.

As there were also those among us who would most certainly pray that if Mankind should fail and fall from grace, and perish at his own will of design and desired effect, and in by doing so, would eventually prove that this outcome would inevitably free us from our servitude and obligations to Humanity in separating the Heavens from the Earth forever, which some Angels also thought and believed would ultimately return and realign us back to God's good grace whilst allowing for his favoritisms to shine upon us once again as his perfect and beloved creation.

As I knew that I had to go in search of the ones that I had up until now only heard rumors of, for since the time that Hark the Herald Angel had been taken up into the highest upper echelons of God's concealment, and Stefan Styles had become indivisible to the countless successions of life upon birth and upon rebirth, and Ophlyn the Herald Angel had all but been removed from the sight of creations beginning and ending for all eternity, then I somehow felt or knew that it should befall upon me to be left to consider the outcome and fate of some the Earth Angels who had become born within the most recent of ages, but as of yet were not yet tested or put through the trials of their abilities in coming forth to be select in this new dawning age of the Empyreans.

And so firstly it was I who was to descend to the place and abode of none other than that of Kali Ma, who had by now given birth and grown the young Earth Angel known as Nephi, so it was that when I had reached and arrived at this holistic and remote place that Nephi I would find for some peculiar notion had already anticipated my coming forth and had come out of his Mother's domain to meet and to greet upon my descent.

Who are you stranger, I am Haven, Nephi, but how do you know my name, because it is written in the Heavens, and are you from such a place in the Heavens, yes Nephi I am from the Empyreans, then you too also knew of my Father, yes I knew Ophlyn the Herald Angel, and what has become of him, your Father has achieved many things Nephi, and his service to God and the Angeldom of the Empyreans is of paramount value and importance, yes I know that as my Mother

has often enough explained that to me and the many revelations of
his acts off often defiance, but tell me Haven, where is my Father
now, Well you Father is no more other than he is removed from
the face of eternity, but why, why is he removed, what did he do to
become stricken from such realities, this much I do not know Nephi,
except that it was God's will, God's will you say Haven, but which
God would take away a Father form his Son, and a Son from his
Father

Well I do not know except that God has a purpose for everything
and everyone in this World and the next Nephi, but why has he done
such a thing if my Father as you say is of such paramount value and
importance to you and the Angels of the Empyreans, I do not know
except that we have our duty and our role to fulfill in an agreement
in God's Kingdom, but I do not know this God, Haven, and I have no
agreement with him, well no perhaps you do not know this Nephi,
but our forbearers did and so that matter stands between you and
God and not you and me, but I have no knowledge of this Haven,
so how can you say this, and why have you come here, I have come
to fulfill my covenant to God and the Angels of the Empyreans and
the Earth, but as I told you I have no covenant with this God, I did
not ask or cause myself to be born into this World of God, so what
is my duty and obligation, why have you come to seek me out and
what is it that you intend to ask of me or to extend to me in the name
of your God and the Empyreans of this Earth, well it is of concern
and worry to me Nephi, that I came here to inquire after you, but on
who's authority, God's.

Well no not exactly, but more of that of the Earth Angels and of that
of which you are a part, but why did not God come in your place if
I am of such importance and value to you all in such a way, because

no one has ever really seen the creator of this world, then how can you claim to know him then Haven, because of faith Nephi, faith you say, but faith in what, what have you seen or witnessed to give you such faith, I have seen many things in a short time Nephi, and so this has caused you to have faith, yes Nephi, I have seen the Archangels and the abiding place of God, but what kind of Angels are these, well they are the most divine and highly ranked Angels Nephi, are they tall like me, no I believe you are taller, are they as strong as me, well I don't know except they're strength is untested but they appear to have a great might, then maybe I should challenge them to see if they are stronger than me.

Well I wouldn't suggest it Nephi, and why not, do you fear them, well yes I fear them a little, then you are not fit to be an Angel, there are many kinds of Angels Nephi not just to fight or to kill or to destroy, but if I were to fight these Archangels do you think I could crack their skulls wide open, well perhaps you could Nephi I do not know your strength or your abilities, well that is good, perhaps you shall discover them one day Haven.

So you say that the name Nephi, my name, is written in the Heavens, then what does it say about me, well it says that you are a Hero and Warrior, but how can such a thing be said of Nephi, when I have played no part on warranted no merit for these things to be mentioned about me, well Nephi, I think it is because of the Legacy of the Nephilims and the Nephilites that these things have also be admitted and attributed to you for the sake of your Angelic Father Ophlyn.

The Nephilites you say, and they were great warriors you say, but what became of them, well many of them are only spoken of as

Clive Alando Taylor

Legends, but ultimately they were referred to as the Fallen Sons
of God, well it would seem that your coming here has only so
far brought insult to me and my Father's legacy Haven, have you
nothing good or wise or pleasing to tell me of this Angeldom, well
yes Nephi, but it may not please you to hear of things that may
distort what we truly are, and that because of our calling, some of us
have a greater calling than even ourselves to fulfill, if it is God's will
then for those of who agree to maintain our file, rank and position
will do and remain to do so, but what of those that defy God and
do not hold such faith in high esteem, well as I said Nephi, even the
greatest of us can become fallen at any time in our ability to pursue
our individual choices, as we in truth are all free agents in God's
Kingdom to choose and do as we will, well now I am beginning to
like you a little bit more Haven, as I believe that I am a so called free
agent in this so called Kingdom of God.

Just then Kali Ma came outside to meet us, Haven how are you it's
good to see you again, as always it is also good to see you too Kali
Ma, and greetings to you Earth Mother Kali Ma, as you might not
be aware but much has happened since we were last together, well
as an Earth Mother I am aware that things are always in a state of
transition, but I see that you are somehow different, and that you
have changed and matured much more Haven, yes Kali Ma it is true,
over time I have evolved you could say, but also I would like to offer
my deepest sympathies concerning the Herald Ophlyn your beloved
and consummate, well it is with great acceptance and compassion
that I am grateful for your sympathies, but I sense and feel and know
that his Spirit in presence still lingers and is also here with me, so
do not be alarmed and surprised at me and my Angel Child, as you
can see that Nephi is his own person, and very much like his Angelic
Father.

14

But tell me why have you come here now Angel Haven, well I have come because as you may be aware that the relationship is changing and advancing or declining depending on how you look at it, well yes Haven as an Earth Mother I am very much attuned and aware of many things, but I feel that you are about to take my Son from me for some purpose, well I have only come to ask if he will abide with me, but why, how can my Son already take charge of matters concerning Heaven, when he is not yet fully mature, well I am sure that he will change and evolve very soon Kali Ma, but moreover I need him to accompany me to find another, and who is this other, I am not so sure, as I do not know everything concerning this offspring, but as you may be aware that Mankind and Humanity is suffering great losses because of their choices and forced errors upon this Planet, yes I aware that we are suffering unto our own destruction, but how can that be helped when perhaps God has turned his back on us,

I am not sure if God has done such a thing unto creation, as we must all bare some responsibilities for our actions, as much as this Angeldom and the Earth Mothers also have a duty to respond and to act in such a crisis of desperate times, well yes Haven, but since the last Judgment and Harvest the role of the Earth Mothers has dwindled in response, yes but I believe that perhaps there is one Angel who can prevent this misfortune from becoming a detrimental outcome for us all, then tell me what do you want to know, I need to know if there was a consummate child born between Papiosa and the one from the Celestial Abode Angel Leoine, well as far as I know that may well be true or not, except that I am not so sure, but if it were possible then only the Angels of the Celestial Abode could know such a thing, but how would it be possible for a Celestial Angel and a Man of Earth to be able to conceive such a Being, as it is near enough an impossible act.

Well yes perhaps it is, as I know of no divinity conceived in such a way, but if somehow she had become Human before her consummation then wouldn't it be possible that way, well yes if she had become Human, then yes, but what of the offspring, wouldn't that child be Human or an Angelic creation to a greater or lesser degree, I see, what you mean Haven, so you want Nephi to accompany you, yes I do, But I cannot fly, no matter Nephi, we can travel as Humans do until the time of your true Birth, very well Mother, I shall attend with Haven, if you must, then you have my blessing, but please do not cause Heaven to move against him or hold him in any contempt because of his Father Ophlyn, Haven, I will not allow it Kali Ma, we shall only seek out the other to see and learn if this matter of reality can be halted, then go and Godspeed be with both of you.

As even in our endeavors to push on and to discover and to uncover the true mystery surrounding the rumor if indeed Papiosa and Angel Leoine had indeed conceived of an Angelic Earth Child, it would also be that unbeknowingly at that time that the Fallen ones had already gathered themselves together if only to speedily hasten the fall of Man's sight God and from the Kingdom of the Heavens, which would inevitable throw the Empyreans into some kind of revolt and chaos, as once again it would please the forces of darkness to preside and watch over and witness the separation of Heaven and Earth and the demise and downfall of Mankind of his own despicable fashioning whilst causing and creating Humanity to suffer in such a and disgraceful catastrophic way.

As it had been given over to Asmodeus and six others, Sammael, Lilith, Ahriman, Balan, Baliel and Molloch to take charge and to lead a prevailing force and advance against the Empyreans, in order to gain influence and to wage War if necessary, if only to cause dissent and to cause the disaffected Angels to rise up and to take part in such cause and effect, in allowing for the Heavens to become completely disrupted, and so it was that as Nephi and I embarked upon our journey to the birth place of Papiosa, that somewhere deep inside of me, I felt the winds of time were rapidly changing towards something more sinister stirring within, or could it be that the time had certainly come where we could no longer avoid the unavoidable, and yet predict the most unpredictable outcome that could and would take place, which was a War in the Heavens itself.

Eventually when we arrived somewhere in a remote village in Africa, we seemingly began to be overcome by an atmospheric feeling of elation and joy and happiness, as if the land in itself, were of the nature of a pleasant and very abundant and plentiful peace, as everyone seem to be of a kind and pleasing nature, as these villagers and town dwellers were somewhat spiritually fulfilled in their natural habitat of green pastures, and so as we entered therein I inquired within if anyone knew of the Man Papiosa, Yes Papiosa, as they took me by the hand and led me through and past a stream teeming with life, as there was in our midst a Girl who looked at me and smiled as myself and Nephi passed her by and were brought to a simple but makeshift dwelling, where they pointed at the open archway and said Papiosa lives here.

And so in raising my voice ever so slightly I called out his name, Papiosa, and in matter of moments a elderly man approached me at the doorway, who is it that calls the name of Papiosa, it is I Haven and Nephi the Son of Kali Ma, and with that response he raised his eyes to stare upon for us for what seemed like an eternity, Haven Son of Simeon, yes I replied, and Nephi, but who and what is Nephi, I am the Son of Ophlyn, astonishing he said upon remark, Ophlyn has a Son, but how, well it is a long story Papiosa, come, come inside and sit and talk with me some more about long stories, and so we entered in and sat with Papiosa, come we must drink and eat a little as he invited us to do so, but I cannot eat Papiosa, but why, because I am not of this realm, therefore I cannot become stained and tainted by it, Oh yes I remember, you are an Empyrean, but what of you Nephi, of course I would like to eat if you don't mind Papiosa, and for a moment we all laughed together, until the Girl also entered in to join us, Oh this is my Daughter replied Papiosa, her name is Anahita.

Anahita, just then a ghostly whisper seemed to quietly fill the room, we must compete the circle, but it was if we did not at first notice it within the consciousness or surroundings of our enclosure or reality, but it seemed to alarm Nephi, what did you say, I said her name is Anahita, no I mean what did she say, I said nothing she replied, but I thought I heard you say something, well you did not Nephi, but how do you know my name, because you mentioned it to my Father as you entered here within, so then Nephi smiled once again and began eating the food that Papiosa had provided for us, so tell me what of Heaven Haven, and what of Love today that you can both tell me about, well there is much to tell Papiosa, but it seems that the world stands still here, as if nothing affects you, well that is because of Anahita, her birth has brought good fortune and prosperity and contentment to this place, but how, because of God, replied Papiosa, because God is pleased with her, and so are we, as a matter of fact, and so is the entire village, we have suffered much here in the past, but Anahita has brought us into God's good hands.

I see but where is your Wife, Oh she wanders around and about freely, she is also a good spirit among us, I think we have more the two of blessings, because of God's greatness, but tell me why have you come to seek out Papiosa, well to not be to insulting or impolite towards you Papiosa, I believe that Anahita is the reason why we have come to inquire after you, but my daughter but why, what do you want with her, well the truth is the people Papiosa, the people are suffering, they are suffering in such a way that it is destroying themselves, so you think my daughter can ease their prolonged suffering, well yes and much more, as you said yourself, since she was born in your village, well everything is just like a paradise.

Yes it is, that is why you cannot take her away from us, no Papiosa, we don't want to take her away, we just need her help, just then another whisper filled the room, to complete the circle, and so as it did Nephi stopped eating and looked directly at Anahita, I'm sorry, for what, well I thought you said something, no I did not, Oh Ok then, then she laughed as if Nephi was being silly and appeared to be a little bit confused, but how can she help you, then all of a sudden Leoine walked in and joined the conversation, because they want her to save the world and to prevent another harvest, What! Said Papiosa, but how is this possible, when will this happen, well Papiosa, I believe that it is already happening, but she is my only child, what can she do to go up against the foes of Heaven, she is also my child too Papiosa, spoke Leoine, and she bears the gift of a Thousand Earth Mothers if not more, be silent Leoine, but it is true my love, she was born to save the world, just then we all became silent and looked at Anahita who was just smiling.

Upon their approach towards the Heavens, it would seem that Asmodeus and the six others had already caused the alarm call of the Trumpeter to be a sounded in the Empyreans, so they would be immediately and instantly met by the Guardians of the Door, who upon the intervention had instructed to Asmodeus to go back and return forth to the Underworld from which they had so hastily sprang from in beginning their ascent, Give us our rites of passage Guardians, so that we may be heard on account to give and add our measure of sanction and terms concerning this place and the Worldly domain of the Earth, No! for you are the banished ones form this place and you have no leverage or merit or terms of proposing or bargaining with which to plead and to satisfy the Angeldom, for there is none amongst who is permitted to sanction or dictates any terms to those who reside alongside that which is fulfilled, beyond that it cannot and shall not be allowed or be consented or for any of you to abide, or to even give counsel, or to the engaged or to be heard and listened to by any of the Empyreans from those of you that are from the depths of the Fallen Ones of that the other place.

Then you shall feel the Might and the Wrath of our Swords if you do not allow us passage Guardian, No! as it is you that shall be forced once again to become assigned and exiled into the Abyss of your imprisonment, well it would seem that those amongst you are unaffected and less concerned and caring and compassionate about the potential death of those the inhabitants of this decaying Earth, of course we are concerned, but as long as the Earth has become your playground of ruination for far too long Asmodeus, as it seems now that you would have History accept and believe that God had somehow turned his back on his Creation.

But alas he has Guardian, for where is your God now, as even now we have come thus far with no direct judgmental force set upon us, because it is I and not God that shall hold you to account where you stand, just then Sammael, Lilith, appeared from behind Asmodeus, and had managed to gain advantage over the Guardian by the art of surprise, and so it was that they would be caused to restrain and subdue the Guardian, until Ahriman, Balan, Baliel and Molloch could forcefully breach their passage way into the Heavens that led forth into the Empyreans, although the Guardian was not killed or destroyed, still he fell where he stood, and so Asmodeus was able to gain further access into the Angeldom of the Empyreans.

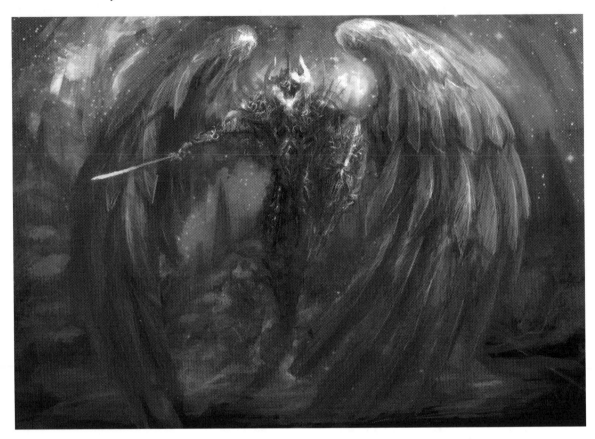

But once it was written and recorded by Pablo Establo Estebhan Augustus Diablo the Immortal One, that in the book of the Unwritten Laws pertaining to Heaven, that once a Fallen Angel of the Underworld had entered into the Heavens of the Empyreans that they would forfeit and lose all wisdom and strength and knowledge of capability and understanding and comprehension of this place, quite simply because they would not know the inner workings and fundamental structure and influences of the foundations that comes to make up the whole of the Heavens, and so as Asmodeus and the six others were by now not aware that they were becoming weakened and powerless the closer and closer they became to this sacred and holy abode, still as they ventured deeper and deeper within to this vast and complex place to challenge in their arrogance and ignorance their contempt of all the Empyreans.

Meanwhile back in the dwelling place of Papiosa who was still somewhat reluctant to allow for his only Daughter Anahita to play any part in assisting us, in what would possibly become the restoration and the healing of Mankind and Humanity, although up until now none of us knew exactly what it was that should take place and transpire between them to fulfill such an outcome and contract of agreement, but Papiosa as you have said, that not so long ago, that this was a place of unimaginable suffering and famine and desolation, and yet now it has become transformed, so just imagine what Anahita's spirit could bring to the rest of Humanity if indeed she were to make her presence felt.

But how it possible for one such as She, to bring such great harmony and justice and balance and peace and stability on such a grand scale to the rest of Mankind, well I do not know exactly but perhaps she as Leoine has said, in possession of the power of Thousand Earth Mothers if not more, the Papiosa turned to face his Daughter, and took hold of both her hands and looked into her eyes sincerely, tell me Daughter do you know what it is that must be done to fulfill such a bargaining and contract as these two Angels here have mentioned here this day.

And so it was that Anahita became silent, but as she did, Nephi began to squirm and writhe in pain and agony as if something had overcome him but at this point Nephi started perspiring and then sweating pefuriously, as if he were infected by some sort of feverish and tremendous sickness in the heat, he was becoming hotter and hotter, until he could no longer stand the intensity or the effects of heat inside the enclosure that we were dwelling in, and so as Nephi started ripping at his shirt while Papiosa and Leoine and Angel Haven and Anahita stood back and looked on as the metamorphosis of the changing and the knowing had begun, and so it was that Nephi could hardly keep his balance and was by now becoming more and more confused and disorientated.

As such was the sound ringing in his ears which became louder and louder, and seemed somewhat familiar but deafening to Nephi, as it was the fanfare of the horns which resounded in the heavens, as it was now apparent in Nephi's mind, now found to be assuring him for once and for all of what it was that he was to do, and of whom and what he was to become, and of what the reason and purpose of his being was to be, as this calling into Angelhood would profoundly affect all concerned, what's happening, to me I feel strange, do not struggle Nephi, for it is the knowledge's that has begun to take effect upon you, yes it is the beginning and the first signs of your Angel rebirth.

And so it was that the sounds of Nephi's voice began to change to a very high pitch note, as if it were the sound of a voice live Baby trying to communicate for the first time, as he began to roll around on the ground, whilst arching his back as he began having fits, and then began convulsively shake violently, as he tried to gasp for air, then slowly in a half naked state, his wings began to break through from the sides of spine, and for the first time signs of brilliant white feathers began appearing on his back, growing faster and longer by the second, and so it was that without cause, but with quick and natural instincts, Anahita sprang to his aid and placed her hands upon Nephi's back and removed the Seal which was set there by Ophlyn the Herald Angel when Nephi was but a mere Baby, and so it was that as this Seal was removed, the knowledge had begun, and slowly but surely, Nephi had by now gained some sense and stability as he eventually stood to his feet looking both noble and tall and a tower of strength and beauty with a wing span of twelve feet or more.

But because Anahita was the one to remove the Seal, then so it was to b be that it would result in having a strange effect of consequences upon Nephi, the knower, of millions of thoughts and images that had by now flashed and raced through his mind, but as they did it became evident to Nephi that these knowledge's were not so much of the past, but of the future present and the future prevailing, and of these things that had not yet taken place, or at least events that had not yet happened to shape or influence time itself, would unfold and become evidently presented to him, as if nature and humanity may not even have happened at all, and yet it was as if Nephi had become the revealer of a future that he himself had somehow already lived through.

What did you see Nephi, and what do you know of the things to come, well I am not so certain except that the future has somehow presented itself to me in such profound way, although it would seem that from the tell tale signs and the energy forces around me, that I am in receivership of that which I am also becoming aware that you

Anahita, daughter of Papiosa and Leoine, also know of that what
I am, and yet in knowing she does not yet choose to acknowledge
what is the reason why I am revealed, but as the seventh sense and
the insight into that which thou art, and of that which she is she, of
which of that which is of the blessed spirit of the tetra, I see now, I
see that now is not the time to speak or to be concerned with such
things, as Heaven is already under threat and has become breached
by the transgressions of the Fallen ones, and we must take leave
to attend its matters, No! Nephi you stay here and let me go, as
something tells me that you should remain here with Anahita, and
so it was that I Haven once again took to flight homeward bound
towards the Empyreans.

As it was in my departure and absence that Anahita and Angel
Nephi were left to talk to one another, you have seen the future
haven't you Nephi, as you know I have seen many things but I do not
know if it is the future, but tell me why did you choose not to admit
the words that I heeded in your whispers, because I wanted to be
certain, certain of what, of what you were to become, and now that
you have seen and witnessed what I have become, why did you not
admit that it was a voice inside of you which spoke out in silences,
because it is not me, then who is it.

I think you may have an idea of who it is, but how can I know
except that it came from you, then look into your heart and mind
and tell me what you see, well I say to you now I have seen many
things that may or may not be true, then tell me what is true, is it not
true that you are beautiful Anahita with the power of a Thousand
Earth Mothers, but that is of no consequence, as I believe that you
have War in your Soul Nephi, well perhaps I do but that is also of
no consequence, Oh but it is Nephi, if you already know what will

happen tomorrow or the next day, or even next year and the years that follow, but what do you mean Anahita, I mean if you choose to go to War then ultimately all that you will ever see and adhere to in this life and the next is the ravages of War.

So what are you saying that I should not go to War, when War is declared in the Heavens, no Nephi I am saying nothing, except that you can choose whichever path extends and lends itself to you, but if you go to War, then I shall not know of what consequence shall befall us all, and what consequence is that, it is the fate of the World that brought you here to me is it not, and now you would jeopardize and throw that all away, and in by doing so, Man also does to himself and becomes the destroyer of the things he so loves so much, but what of love and War Anahita are they not one of the polarisation, no they are Nephi, but what would you have me do, if I do not ascend to the Empyreans to fight and aid and assist my kindred Angels then what shall I do, as I told you and as I will now tell you again, only one who is not of the mind and the soul and the spirit of War can fulfil the things that you have come to seek out upon this time of Judgement.

So it is the purity that you speak of and mention in my sight, and are you not now so pure upon your rebirth, well that I am, but I must also return to Heaven, No you do not, you only think you do because you want to fight, but do you not think that Heaven has seen and witnessed these things before, and whether your presence there shall really change the course of History or not over the Earth and Mankind, well perhaps not, but if I stay here then what shall my life become, it shall become fruitful and abundant, but how can you say this, because it is not me that says the silent words but another, look Anahita I have no time for games and second guessing, very well then follow your heart and your desire, and I shall follow mine, if you persist in this War of the Heavens, then soon there shall be no Heaven for us, but why do you make such statements, are we not one with the Heavens, only one who does not have War inside of him can complete the circle.

And with that statement Angel Nephi knew what Anahita meant by her stark choice of words, and in a way even though he had no fear in his heart, still it frightened him to hear Anahita speak this way, I now know what you mean, but do you, yes I do, but something tells me that I must now take to flight, but where will you go, I don't know but I must extend my wings and go somewhere, but if I do not return so soon, do not worry or be concerned after me, as I am at opposite spectrums of the days of revelations coming to pass, then go where you will Angel Nephi,

But just before Angel Nephi took to flight, Leoine appeared at the door with a Bow in her hand, Nephi take this with you, but what is it for, it is the Bow of Nimrod, for whosever shall shoot and fire this Bow into the Heavens shall begin the integration and emergence of the Angels of the Empyreans and that of the Celestial Abode, and shall also in by doing so, become the appointed one at God's right hand, and so Nephi took the Bow from Leoine, and with that Angel Nephi took to flight within the skies, and ascended away and beyond the sight of Anahita and Leoine and Papiosa.

As such it was that Angel Nephi was now betwixt between being held by the virtues of Anahita, and yet to aspire and to ascend to the Heavens to see and witness what calamity may be awaiting to befall upon the Angels of the Empyreans, but what did Nephi also begin to experience within these transcendental thoughts, which were by now weighing up his brow and becoming a burden upon the purity of his Heart, and also now stirring within his soul, was what he should also do to resolutely meet and deal with these troubling and arising matters, in that he himself knew were not originally because of himself but because of Anahita, but as to whom did he think or believed that he owed or his allegiances were too, were now an opposing contradiction, as to whom or what he had now thought of what he had become.

As such was the symptoms of the beauty and immediate and sincere attraction for Anahita now becoming strangely born inside of him, but also there was the heed of the call of the challenge to lean towards the fight or the flight of the Empyreans, although deep down he already knew what was his truth and what was to become error if he so chose to move against it, and yet even below in the infernal regions of that which he could now also sense, was also the forces of darkness gathering itself together, as none other than those the fallen ones, who were by now ready to arise and to ascend in support and to bring reinforcement to also aid Asmodeus and the six others who had already by now breached Heavens threshold.

As so it was to be that the lesser of the fallen Angels led by Samyaza and Arstikapha, along with nineteen others of which were, Armen and Kakabael, Turel and Rumyel, Danyal and Kael, and Barakel, Azazel and Armers, Bataryal, and Basasel, Ananel and Turyal, Simapiseel, and Yetarel, and Tumael and Tarel, and Rumel and Azazyel, who were becoming readily prepared to also ascend out of the Abyss and extend their reach into the Heavens and beyond, as it may have by now become the consequence that they in themselves could deliver the final blow in separating and dividing the realm that stands as the dwelling place of the Earth Angels.

And so it was to be that upon this the threshold of the Empyreans, it would be my Father Angel Simeon that would first appear and present himself and come forth to meet with and to acknowledge Asmodeus, where is Hark the Herald, Angel Hark is no more Asmodeus, no more, Asmodeus begins to laugh to himself, it would seem that there have been many changes and successors in my absence of this place, as I see that even Hark has come to abandon this place of presiding influence, believe what you will Asmodeus but I am here in presence to turn you around and to turn you away and back to the place from which you have come, turn around, turn away, is that how you greet your fallen adversaries, as you can see I have not come this far to be turned around, if fact from where I now stand, I believe that it is you and the abode of the Angels that should turn around and abandon this dream of the Angels babies and join us and together with Satan we shall rule the World and all the Heavens that it encompasses.

Nay Asmodeus it cannot nor shall not be so, as it is written.., Written! Written where, and by who, the Hand of God, even you and I know that God holds us all in contempt of the mere truth that we are what we are and all that will ever be, you should turn your back on him in an instant and release yourselves from this bondage of servitude and Will of slavery, nay Asmodeus it is you and that those that follow you that are the slaves of Hell, Asmodeus begins to laugh, it would seem that God and Satan are both not too dissimilar in their nature upon this Kingdom, as both are hardly distinguishable one from the other don't you think Simeon, but then again you are not permitted to think in such a unique and individualistic fashion are you Simeon.

Say what ill of me you shall Asmodeus, but as of you, you have no freedom, as your inheritance shall always be that of abysmal infernal hell that you shall occupy for all eternity, and neither I nor shall the Angels of Empyreans become drawn into the darkness of ages that you so insist upon spilling out and above and over the Earth, then you leave us no alternative Simeon, as even now upon the edge of darkness had prevailed, as the fallen ones shall come creeping up upon you and remove those of you that shall not denounce your pledges of allegiance to the Almighty, and fall down now and bow to me in the name of Satan, allow me to say this Asmodeus, that if you persist and I must reiterate for you and your own ignorant and arrogant unperceivable nature, that what is written shall come to pass, and that you and those of the scourge that you command, shall be bound for all eternity and thrown into the lake of fire and brimstone for all the nations to see that you have tricked and deceived them in your poisonous revolt to inflict in your vain attempt to overcome the Angels of Heaven.

And with that Asmodeus retreated back a little bit of the way in acknowledging that not all was quite in his favour, but also becoming cautious so as to see who else would come into view to support and to aid Simeon upon this single moment of imminent battle, and also in realising and becoming aware, that the further away they were from the Abode of the Angels, and the closer they were towards the gravity of Earth, that they indeed would retain a large portion of their strength and ability to strike an engaging attack upon their adversaries, and sure enough from behind Angel Simeon did a small handful of Empyrean Angels, which did encircle around and about the Heavens above, guardedly watching and observing in anticipation of the six fallen ones that had by now come alongside Asmodeus to wait and prepare for their moment of engagement.

And so it was to be that upon my arrival and not a moment too soon, that I did also see the reinforcements of the lesser fallen ones led by Samyaza and Arstikapha, also now come to arrive at almost the same time as myself upon this finite moment in time, and with their sudden arrival, were the Swords of the fallen drawn and given the command to commence into battle, as also too did my Father Angel Simeon also give the order to retaliate and defend all that the Empyreans stood for, and it was fought through with the clashes of metal and steel, and the dominance to ultimately overpower and relieve one to the other of the ethereal breath of life, as such was the onslaught of the masses of Angels that the confusion and the chaos ensued, and so I couldn't think except but to help, even though I had to act in accordance with the scriptures, but as of yet I was not born nor prepared for the fight of any battle, but this was my home and my place of sanctuary, so how could I not fight to defend and keep the enemy at bay from this realm without boundaries.

And so I entered therein into the midst of the fight, and in by doing so put myself at risk from being killed and destroyed by the foes of the Empyreans, and yet I felt the lifeforce increase inside of me, as if I were empowered with the strength of a hundred or more Angels, and so I fought with fear and courage at my side, until I was exhausted and gasping for breath and in by becoming so, I was knocked to a state to semi consciousness, whist watching all about me become as blur to my eyes, but if I were to have one vision, then it was to see An Angel come to my aid and raising me up from the place of where I fell, and once again to stand and gain my conviction, as it was Nephi that had appeared to me with whom I was so pleased and happy to see.

Haven, we do not have much time, but I think I now know the future, but what do you mean you know the future Nephi, is this not the future that we are now fighting for, No! Haven, I must not and cannot fight this fight with you, well not today anyway, but why not Nephi I thought you wanted to crack some skulls, well yes perhaps I do, but not today, today I must do what is right not just for myself but also for you and all concerned, but what is it Nephi what must you do, nevermind now Haven, just take this Bow, it is the Bow of Nimrod, as it will defeat your enemies and bring about a restoration of the Heavens, but fire it whenever, wherever your heart speaks and tells you to take aim and fire the Bow.

And so it was for a moment that the fighting had disengaged as the fallen ones were by now regrouping, as too did we Angels of the Empyreans also regroup besides one another, and then Asmodeus looked into our direction and pointed to Angel Nephi, you there, who and what are you, I am Nephi, Nephi, yes Nephi, but are not the Nephilites fallen and stricken, yes they are, then why do you stand with the Empyreans, come join us upon this day that we shall wreak havoc upon the Heavens, nay I cannot join you, nor can I join the Empyreans upon this day, what are you cowardly and afraid and fearful of your God, nay I neither cowardly nor afraid, then come tell me what are you, I am Nephi of the Nephilites, and once again I am risen, and with that short exchange Nephi once again took to the skies and had disappeared within the same instant that he had appeared, and so too did the battle recommence, and so too did the fighting begin once again.

And so it was to be that we could not have anticipated that during this struggle with Asmodeus and his reinforcements, that also the Scourge would also come to rise up against us, as such was the blackened and deadly nature of these demons desecrated with neither spirit nor soul, would cause us to alarm, and so I was feeling quickened and eager to shoot the bow into the midst of these creatures, except that a green mist did come to drift into the air and around and about us, in that with all its intensity for a moment it did cover us over everywhere, although it was upon its fading and disappearance that we did see coming forth from out of it, the Seven Archangels Gabriel, Michael Raguel, Raphael, Remiel, Uriel and Zerachiel, who were by now descending upon the Scourge and destroying and severing them at will ferociously, and so I paused to execute my judgement, as by now I felt that the words that Nephi spoke to me, in saying that I should use my heart and not my head as to when was the right time to shoot and fire this Bow that I had now found to be clutching in my possession.

As it was that with this Bow in my hand that I did not truly know of its significance except that the Legacy of this Angeldom that had been revealed to me, that God had indeed separated the People from one to the other simply because Nimrod had once fired and shot it to strike and pierce at the Heavens and towards the highest pinnacle in proving that the Kingdom of Heaven could be reached and proven in its fulfilment, but perhaps it was that such a ubiquitous and omnipotent nature had overcome me, in that I did not wish or want it to be proved and realised in its own purposing of revealing to me or to any us, as to what is the true nature and composition of what Man had come to define and call and yet hardly recognise as God in the Being or the reason and the force behind all totality.

And yet Angel Nephi who could so easily have championed this cause, had now left and put this truth and responsibility upon my bearing, and yet what would be the consequence if I fired and shot

this Bow at my enemies striking at Heavens threshold, as such was
the ensuing battle that raged between the Angels of the Empyreans
and the fallen ones, then was this to be as in the days of Old, where
the Victors of this battle as in the War of Sheol, would have to
become true and sincere and virtuous over the rights of Mankind
and Humanity, or was this to be the breaking and the dismantling of
the Heavens, where the Angels would indeed become separated from
Mankind for all eternity

As also upon my reflection, that in the company of Papiosa that my
ears and my heart did also hear and heed the words through the
silences of Anahita, even though I chose not to acknowledge her,
in that somehow the circle were somehow or somewhat incomplete,
but why was Anahita so personal so as not to reveal the true inner
spirit and voice that resounded within and around her, even though
we kept good faith and good company, and so as I pulled back the
Bow of Nimrod and took aim, as the Archangels had more or less
defeated the Scourge that had for a time come upon us, as such
was the nature of the Heavenly Being, that Asmodeus and the six
others along with Samyaza and Arstikapha along with the other
nineteen, did realign themselves so as to counter the offence of the
Archangels.

And such was their positioning, that all twenty eight of them were
now grouped together, and so it was to be that at this specific
moment, that I shot and fired the arrow into the midst of their
grouping, as such was its force that all the Heavens shook with
thunder and lightning that had now begun to flash in all its majestic
brightness, so much so, that even the Archangels were somewhat
thrown back and off balance, as the rising Sun of the new day that
would come to signify the rising of the Golden Dawning, had come

so close to where we stood and circled above, in that it would now consume all and everything in its path, as was by now beginning to pull Asmodeus and the remaining fallen ones into the very central region and core of its solar system, in that it had also heralded in a new day, as the interaction and the emergence of the Heavens had also begun, in that it had ignited and caused the Celestial Heavens and that of the Empyreans to move and together and to merge in becoming one closer body and union in its reconfiguration.

As such was the vengeance and reproach of the fallen ones, who were by now extinguished and sentenced to an everlasting imprisonment within the infernal and central embodiment of the newly arising Sun, which was by now found to be gloriously shining and standing high above the place where our Battle had taken place, but as for the Archangels and upon their ascent in leaving and departing from us towards the higher points of a place where once I had witnessed the presence of God in all his might, did they commend to grant us with gratitude and appreciation for not allowing the Midheavens to become perturbed and disrupted and given over to the darkness's and the recklessness of the fallen ones.

Even though it was to become pronounced forever more and once again amongst all of this chaos and causality that had by now changed everything in its development, which was to now redefine and change our future relationship with God as well as with that of the Celestial Angels, so basically we would have to start again by forging new alliances with one another, in that we would have to renew our covenant and affirm our promises which was to be defined our fundamental and constructural relationship with the least of God's creation, which was that of the species and the inhabitants of the Earth which was that of Mankind and Humanity.

As it was only in their failed attempt and aims and purpose of commandeering and imposing such a Will upon the people of the World if only to bring about their own downfall and destruction and ruination, that God would turn away from Mankind and Humanity, but such is the verity of God against the transgressions and the violations of the fallen ones, in that it would prove to work against them, as it could not, nor would not prevail to be or even become so, as such was the gravity of this new beginning and of those that would now come forth to draw up the constitutional matters of agreement to further the Will and the reconfiguration between the emergence of the two Heavens, and of that which was by now quickly moving and merging together as one infinite body of which holds the very fabric la tissues de la vie and the essence of the strands that tie the universe together.

As this was to also prove to be integral in forming and supporting both the mid and the lower Heavens which in turn ties the Heaven and the Earth together as well as beyond and below into the lower depths of creation, but as for now, and for those of us who had already survived and outlasted the trials of this battle, took to rest in taking refuge within the higher regions so as to replenish and to sustain our feverish bodies, and to watch the Sun eventually set itself as a sign upon our sights of this our most infinite hour, as such was this beckoning horizon that could only seem to suggest to us, that we were still not yet fully proven or confident of that which we believed to be certain, or at least to be sure of the way, until the establishment of this new dawn that we had now come to know, would come to signify and be seen and witnessed as the newly arising Star or Sun of Nejeru.

For even as we are all called into account one by one to be heard by those that once were Heralded within the Southern and the Northern aspects of our coming forth from the Spirits and the Stars, which were pronounced forth by the infinity of dark matter, as we were once again determined that through the choices of our consequence, that albeit that we had to take strength and sustenance from our firm footing within the Empyreans, we also now had to seek once again, and to inquire within the spirit of our nature, as also within the Wisdom of the Elders of the several worlds, who only seem to consciously communicate with us through the collectiveness of the patheia, and with some degree of patience coupled with that of a practical and simple matter found to arising out of the consciousness of the universe.

For their very essence of their respective positioning and timeless thoughtfulness is knowledge personified, for they are not thinking, as they have already thought, and they are not feeling, for they have already felt, except that they are still very much aware of that which is both the constructs of the pillars of the birth and the inception caused by the fertile conception that is brought through to the transitions of all infinite causality, as that which comes forth from out of the root of the tree of life, if not the highest echelons, and of that which is of the upper most and inner sanctums that we all adhere and abide to, within that part of Heavens creation itself is notably so, that their very Being is very much the source and the energy, and of that which is the substance of that which is found not only to be engaging within itself, but also in realising in that which has already been realised, and yet as they are already aware of that which they are continuously informing us of, then to whom else shall they declare it to within and extended through their Being, if not beyond the Heavens and the Earth itself, when they too have already been permitted enough to keep us all informed infinitely of such things throughout the course of our trials, as the only thing that can be permitted to sit or stand or become constructually influential outside the laws of creation is the creator himself, and the spirit of life, esprit de corps, at the core of the spirit.

As each one of us in turn are affected by a common cause and call to life, if not for ourselves then for each other, as we are not so independent of what is the tree of life, no matter the action or the choices that we are all affirmed to uphold or to distinguish as choice, as such is the virtue of each Angel within this Angeldom, in that we are all instantly influenced by each other, as such was the choice of Angel Nephi who had by now returned to the habitat of Papiosa in seeking once again to eagerly know more, and to learn more of this feeling of expression and admiration born out of an innocent affection for what would be, the becoming of the Earth Mother Anahita, as when Angel Nephi did indeed behold and see her again, it was then that they both of them in seeing each other did in fact come to know that it was to be so.

I see you have returned to me from flight so I can only assume that you did not have cause to fight in the endless engagement of battle of trials and tribulations, yes it is true, even though I am a warrior, I do not know why I did not endure unto my Will, but I believe that this would have become predictable and expected of me, do you think Heaven will remember my name if not for the War that I did not attend to fight, yes Nephi, Heaven will remember that you chose a superior destiny, a superior destiny, but tell me Anahita what is that, it is the future of this world, but how can that be when life is so timid and fragile, I mean we may save the world momentarily, but soon the inevitable shall come to pass, yes perhaps but the human being is very resourceful and may even one day out do us all, then I shall wait to see if man can learn to fly and reach the Heavens if only to carve out his name upon the tree of life without help assistance from anything or anyone,.

You are very amusing Nephi, and so too are you Anahita, I think that you are right mankind shall always need the inspirations that such deities can bestow upon their heads and hearts, but what about your heart Nephi, now that you cannot fight and brag and boast of your strength and victories in battle what shall you do, I shall do nothing Anahita, except that I have a distinct feeling that you awaiting upon me to fulfil destinies calling out to you if not me, well yes perhaps it is true, but I wish that you shall say what is in your heart for me Nephi, but I do not know my heart, for we are young and foolish in our hearts, as such is the human part of our feelings.

Then let us become like the humans and learn to love with all fault and carelessness as we are young and you are younger than I, but how can we, well if you wish and desire me to love as you are, then to you I shall become the beloved, but first you must ask my Mother and Father if they are otherwise opposed or in favour of our agreement in that we are seeking this union of relationship, but how can I ask that when your Father fears that if your presence should leave here, that calamity and desolation may once again befall upon this place.

Trust me and have a little faith in me Nephi, for it shall not be so, for I am also affirmed in the truth and the absolute, as I know that you are also, so do not fear my Father Papiosa for he is only worried of his own fate as you shall come to discover that, then if he is worried why should I add to his anxiety and concerns, because you shall show him that it shall not be so, and what about you Mother, what shall she say concerning this matter, she shall say nothing except in establishing and giving her blessings upon us, then I shall speak to your Father Papiosa as you have instructed me to do, nay Nephi, do not do so under my instruction, do as thou will because you feel and desire it to be so, do as you say, will you not, well yes if I am true to my word, then yes I agree it is true to say that I feel desire for you too Anahita, well good as I am so pleased to hear you say such things.

As it was of the most heartfelt disturbance of feeling and nervous tension, that there was no real convenient moment in time when Angel Nephi could approach Papiosa to hold such a conversation of such a private matter concerning his one and only daughter Anahita, for if it were not for Leoine to see in him that his senses were distressed and overcome with an air of unease, and an undeniable affection which was less than willing to speak so frankly about a language which sprang forth only from the Heart of An Angel now to be found in Love, and so she urged him in a way so as to defend his principles instead, Nephi, a warrior are you not, yes I believe it is said to be so Leoine, and an Angel without fear are you not, well yes I believe myself to be so, then why do you tremble upon entering our abode for a second time, tell me what troubles and disturbs you.

And so it was, that at once Angel Nephi had no words of reply, answer me Nephi, well I have come to speak with Papiosa, then speak Son of Ophlyn, speak, well as you may now know and be aware that I have no words readily available to satisfy you with, except that you may find offence in me for asking, for asking what, for asking that I may come to take Anahita away with me, Away! But where and for what purpose, Wait! My love, can you not see it is love that speaks and not Nephi, but Nephi what do you know of love, I know nothing except my own feeling Papiosa, and so you have learnt nothing of these foolish matters and yet you are so brave and so bold so as to proposition and positing in approaching Papiosa to remove my daughter from my sight, nay Papiosa it is not so, it is because she has already decided that in her own Heart, and so Papiosa has become confused.

Listen to him Papiosa, for she is grown enough to contend to her own affairs and to make up her mind, but what shall become of the foundations and this place that we have now brought into fulfilment, nothing shall change Papiosa, but how do you know that, because Anahita has said it to be so, no matter where we ascend and descend too, this place will remain unchanged, but I fear for her life, her safety, her well being, do you not see me as I am Papiosa, I am Angel, therefore nothing can befall upon her that I cannot defend against, foe or otherwise, very well then tell her to come in here and to speak with me.

He is Angel, he is not Human, he half of one and half of the other, but I love him, as much as your love has been caused to be loved when nothing more and no one could find love in you, and now you want to tell me and to teach me something which is untrue of you, do you love Leoine, but what kind of question is that Anahita, you know that is a question that does not need to be answered, well why do you ask me such questions when you have known it to be so, but what will become of us, Nothing! Nothing will become of you, except what will become of me if I do not abide and go from this place with Nephi, then it is true, that you love an Angel, that has no root, but what is the root if not love, even as you have tried in seeking to underpin God and to find out the root of existence in itself, well Why! And for what reason and what purpose, do you love me Father, yes Anahita, I do with every fibre in soul, then let me be, and we shall find love together, and if you do not child then if I do not find it, then all shall become as it once was, and the land shall not flourish, and the fishes shall not swim, and the sky shall fall upon us all like once before, and the laughter shall turn to tears, and the happiness shall become as sorrow, as once it was before the birth of Anahita.

And so it was that Papiosa was reduced to tears in knowing full well, the time the time had come for Anahita to fulfil her destiny, and in knowing and realising the determination and effort and commitment that it also takes for all things to be and become proven, very well then, Papiosa understands, for it is better for love to flourish, than for a people to suffer in misery, torment, and pain, and loneliness, go with the Angel, and be fruitful and be happy with thyselves besides thy love, and so it was that the first seeds of the marriage of Heaven and Earth would take root and begin once again with the Angel Nephi and with the Earth Mother Anahita.

As such was the air fresh like spring in sustaining and issuing forth an element of newness and in their oneness, coupled with the feeling and the expression of an innocence and fondness to be found in both their hearts and minds, which had by now granted their freedom to find and explore the wondrous affections that ties the lover to the beloved and Heaven to the Earth, but such was the examination of their freedoms, that it would ultimately bring about its own merits of constraints, for freedom and love do not always happily go hand in hand towards extending and lending themselves in achieving and balancing a great union and partnership, whereas freedom is expression, but love is emotion, whereas happiness is fleeting in both its comings and goings, so as to lead them both towards their rightful place within the confines and the constructs of the World at large, except but they were not limited by love or freedom, for their embrace in each other's arms did in turn become fortunate as they turned to one another, if only to attend too, and to fulfil each other's expectations and desires.

Your Mother Nephi, tell me does she care for you as I do, My Mother is always steadfast and concerned about me, but her love is not our love, but when she sees our love, then it will also render her Heart to also be joyous and happy, then we must first go to her, so that she can see me and know me, but why don't we give a moment of time to ourselves, until the return of Haven, then we three shall go to see My Mother Kali Ma, I am happy to be with you my beloved, but what matters of Haven if Heaven is disturbed and now moves at Will as we too also move at will, my will is only to be besides you, as you wish, for that is my Will also.

Then let Haven discover us when the time is right, right for what my love, as we two are now more than strangely acquainted because of Haven, and yet my destiny and future now lies in you besides me, and so you must know my inner most self, but I already see besides yourself Anahita, nay Nephi, you see beauty, but you do not see life, or soul, or spirit, or passion, take me up to the place where Angels sip the dew of the ether of the roaming clouds, and then we can begin to complete the circle, but if you are to fly so high in my arms my beloved, you may lose all sense of consciousness, nay it will not be so for the air has already whispered into my mouth and nostrils, and I feel life surging into me, come we go now, before the clouds drift ahead.

And so it was that Nephi wrapped his arms tightly around Anahita, and extended his wings, and as they opened and gradually and gracefully began to climb and ascent from the place where they stood, steadily climbing higher and higher until the ground below was far from beneath their feet as they ascended to reach the edge of the stratosphere, where Anahita was filled with joy and laughter and becoming giddy and elevated, as they touched upon the mist of the clouds drifting by, where Nephi gave Anahita just enough freedom to sip upon the ether and dew of these cold and misty clouds, as he too did also take a sip, and then as he had freed her arms from his embrace, they both began to kiss, suspended within the air only by the strength and the diligence of Nephi's wings.

And so it was that as they drifted a little and then a little more, until they began their descent and came down slowly within a remote place, where the fresh waters were streaming rapidly against the bank of the shoreline, somewhat decorated with wild flowers, this is the place, Nephi, what about this place, this is the place that I wish for us to consummate our love, but we are outside and it is open to spectacle and observation, nay Nephi it is not so, it is nature and full of life, I remember this place, but how do you remember it my love, because I have dreamt of it, are you not the one Nephi who should see things that never were, well perhaps I can, but I think that it is only in battle that such miracles can happen, then your love it is blind, nay Anahita, I can see you and feel you, and hear you breathe and sigh, it is not my love that is blind, it is the War that is coming to an end that I can no longer see, then forget War and find love and peace here with me now.

And with that expression their consummation had begun, for the flowers had decorated the land, and the waters were to come upon their skin as they moved as one in fulfilling their desires of one another, as they rolled and tumbled until they had become locked and tied within a loving embrace, even as they bathed and breathed in the air in all of its freshness as with an affection and a fashion that they did kiss and caress and lovingly care for each other's bodies, as until their love had yielded itself unto the tender and passionate and yet gentle expressions that they both could intimately share in the creation of the very essence of their being and the creativity of their love making.

Meanwhile old friends had become newly acquainted and yet familiar friends, for since the purge of the underworld and the judgements upon the fallen ones had become pronounced as a sentence since the scourge had been ousted and removed from our place of refuge and sanctuary, then so too it was to be that the Heavens drew ever more closer in its union and mergence, as for now we were to see coming forth from the Celestial Dominion for the first time, the discovery of the Angels that had never before had such an interactive interchange or chance of this the revelation between our domain and theirs, as if a wall of invisibility that once separated all, had become vanished and removed and had simply evaporated between us, and no longer held us to virtuously hold us by too many constraints as once was in our duty to serve and uphold all that the Heavens could call and recognise itself to be.

As did the Angel of Justice and the Angel of Mercy come to appear within our midst, as if by one simple and yet reasonable act, to uncover and to discover that for once and for all, that we were all of an equal status, aligned with one simple purpose and fundamental accord, which is why one would ask why it were not permitably so from the very beginning and instance of time, and yet in being in resign to this very idea that once upon a time, that all things were once separate facets and entities if even at opposite ends of this one polarising spectrum, and yet so it was planted in the tree of all knowledge, that each one maintained and contained within it, its' own idealism, that up until now, that neither one of us had no reason or purpose to find ourselves within reach of the other's realms or inner sanctum and separate and individual place of abode.

Angel Haven, I see that it has begun, yes Justice and Mercy, it has begun then it would undoubtedly be that the World has been granted and extended itself over and given another chance and opportunity to save itself from destruction and ruin, well it would seem that the World is all, and that God does not give up upon his creation so easily, as much as we who not give up on God, but it's such a fragile and futile and remote and lonely place don't you think, well I can only think that Mankind in his own madness must sometimes sit and wonder to consider that same notion and feeling if not concerning God himself, but truly if he were here now in more than just spirit and formless presence, then what do you feel he would say to us now, now, well now that we have also been given over to each other who knows, I mean do you think that perhaps he mirrors his own creation, in being fragile and futile and remote and lonely in this World that he has created for all living and earthly and sentient beings.

Well perhaps once I thought I knew all the fragile and the futile and remote and lonely ways of the creator, and even that of the created, but as of now, I only see things as they are Justice, in that they are simply coming and going, dying and evolving, changing and moving to either a lesser or a greater extent of expansiveness, in that perhaps we in our infinite Hearts and Minds go on into making up the many faceted sides and personalities of those of the things that are also already manifest and personified or even reflected back to us, and perhaps we when we look into the mirror or even beyond and into the abyss, we begin to see a God cloaked and draped in his many forms, then in as much, then such are we in our fragile and futile lonely ways, also to find upon true reflection, a spirit or a soul reflected back to us.

Well that seems and sounds poetically true Haven, but the World is such an untameable and somewhat unpredictable World to inhabit, I suppose that the World is like a child trying to discover its four corners as to what it may as of yet uncover or discover about itself, and whether such clues can yield a prized possession of either a treasure or unlock a secret, as such is the expressions of Mankind to seek out his God for answers to his own becoming, and perhaps the World is unpredictable and grotesque, or just as untameable and yet beautiful thing, but not as of yet ready or prepared for how we choose to maintain or see it.

As we do not truly know it, for who are we, and what are we, if not the servants of something that we also fundamentally at the heart of, as we also frequently from time to time inhabiting and occupying this World in our own comings and goings, and so therefore, if we create a World of beauty then we shall come to know beautiful things, otherwise if we leave the World to be left in its own abandonment, then what is left of us within it, then ultimately we know that creation shall fall and crumble one day for certain, and yet when we have no desire, or response, or feeling or attitude toward it, then so too shall the occupants of the world be left defenceless with no regard and no responsibility to afford towards its keepsake, then this World whether we are here or not, will be a lesser form of itself, as such is the child that is separated from its spirit of information, has nothing left to yearn to aspire to and to inquire and improve upon, if only to be taught to reach out to its inventor or creator, if only to ask the why and wherefore, and to be told time and time again, because you are, because all things are, and therefore all things are justified as why, simply because it is so.

For as of when we forsake the World, then we shall end up forsaking all else, and perhaps God may be convinced that he will or will not begin again, or as in that truth, that he may or may not need for his creation to believe and see his Kingdom as we do, and so all is lost to the ultimate void of nothingness and the density of dark matter, or even as we may dare to bring about our own downfall, or otherwise if we persist to rise to meet these challenges, in knowing and realising that the Master of the House may have set mighty task before us, in that we may aim to fulfil and yet achieve it and yet still but fail, as such is our faith and hope in thinking that we are so much more than we can ultimately see or feel, inasmuch that we ought to try to fulfil in our own becoming to be.

Yes Angel Haven, I see, I see that you are at the right hand of God, in that you a servant and yet a master in this creation, and I see that we must make ways so as to cause this union of the Celestials and the Empyreans to be a great and successful and unified embodiment, as I shall now have cause to call upon all the Celestial Angels to announce and to uphold you as Herald, as such that I find that I am affirmed in you in that you are in genuine accord within this union of the Heavens to be reborn and reignited, but alas please pray and tell me what has become of Angel Stefan and Hark the Heralded One, with whom we so hastily departed company from, well Justice, let me answer you in saying that I cannot be so precise in giving you a response of all totality and reasonable insight and depth of understanding, except that Stefan has returned to the beginning of birth, and Hark the Heralded one, well let us just say that Hark is now at oneness and besides the creator and the master of this house.

Hark, Immortalised, I see, well then in my admittance and in hindsight, I see now that perhaps we should not have fled and departed so prematurely, and perhaps we were evermore ignorant and naive in our many ways of thinking, as I see now that it was our fears of the unknown that perhaps the outcome would not have projected itself to be I suppose of one so naturally filled with such dread and trepidation, as such as to what we thought or did indeed witness and suspected at the time occurring concerning the mysteries of Ophlyn the Herald Angel, nay Angel of Justice perhaps you should not have fled so hastily, but perhaps it was meant to be, in such a way for all things to be fulfilled in its eventful promise.

As even I did not know if I were to ever again return back here safely to this place within the abode of the Empyreans, well then I now see that we can move forward and from beyond this point of matter, yes Justice I am satisfied if I am to become Herald, then let this union from here on be one of great and a successful measure, in that it may bring merit and grant us with much stability and loyalty in our alliance and allegiances.

And so it was that the Angels began to organise and assemble themselves at the behest and request of the Angel of Justice, to gather unto themselves and to form a hierarchy in prospective proximity and proportionate balance and union around that which is I Haven the Herald Angel, and so the motion of movement had begun as the Angels of both the Celestial and Empyreans realigned themselves in bringing about the Second and Third Spheres with in itself gave way to the Lower Dominions that influenced and governed over the lower depths which was the domain of the Earth, reaching far below and beyond that which was formed from the dark matter of space and time.

As the First Sphere was that of which was perpetually the transient place in forming the essence and the fabric of what was the infinite sum of all totality of God and His Archangels, and also bound up with those that were beyond and besides the Ophanim in being that which I and Hark once stood in the presence of, and yet it was to be I instead of the others who was to become expelled and propelled from therein, to now give over counsel and infinite wisdom in the name of praise and of worship in its perfection, and so it was that my Father Angel Simeon did but approach me from amongst the multitudes of the Angels of the Celestials and the Empyreans, and as he did so, he did all but bid and instruct me one thing in saying, I beseech thee my Son, I beseech thee, sing Haven, sing so that we may come into the union of our heavenly household and become exalted with the God of our salvation,

And so it was that as I looked around and about me, that I did lift up my sight to the wondrous glories that had befallen upon my eyes as the new Heavens were forming, and so I did all but inhale the breath of voice into my body and chest, and did all but to release and exhale within a heavily sigh, in that I did begin to pronounce and sing the words, Holy, holy, holy is the Lord of Hosts, for the whole Earth is full of his glory, for no sooner than these words had fallen from my mouth, that I soon became aware and noticed that as I sang, that they were also sung and pronounced forth, by the entire multitude of the Angels of the Celestials and Empyreans also, in that we were all now unified in issuing forth a sound of rapturous glory and splendour like a chorus of Angels resounding throughout.

And so it was that for a brief moment that seemed like an eternity across the expanses of space and time, did a portal but open up from way up high above us, as if the clouds in their formations had given way to the illuminations of an intensity of pure light now to be seen forever reaching beyond from the point where we took note to witness, that through these glorified streams of pure energy beaming down upon us and from within the spheres of the Ophanim and the first Heavens, as such was the immediate intensity of its in penetration right through and beyond the second and third spheres of Heaven, that it was enrapturing those amongst us of the Celestial and

Empyreans, in that it did interactively permeate and did affect and did cause an effect upon all upon its path, in both pinpointing with accuracy upon its direction and journeying through to the elements and the density of the dark matter that encapsulated and encumbered itself around and about us.

As such it was that it did come to serve in proving itself into sustaining and going further and further into the depths of the Earth and beyond and into the infinite realms of life itself,

as such was the witnessing of the immaculate interconnectedness woven into the fabric of all three Heavens now becoming instantaneously aligned into one great universal expansion, as such was this light before us in coming forth from the portal itself, that in an instant, it did all but cease to be in its immediacy as everything became clear and returned once again to as it once was except that all was not to be seen as renewed, and yet as we sung so too did my mind begin to wander as the thought of God and Man transpired within my eternal spirit and being, but also much to the point that I did indeed spare a thought for Angel Nephi and His Beloved Earth Mother Anahita, for I knew that somewhere and somehow that they had met and by now had come together beneath these Heavenly skies to forge and kindle and cement their love for each other.

As I also thought and felt that she too also had a dream in fulfilling her own destiny, as too did Nephi's will give over and way to the dream that was always and only to be the dream of the Angel Babies, for the inner spirit of her concealment had spoken out from within the depths of its hiding place, and although I knew not this voice of reason, but what I did sense and feel and come to know was that this spirit had influenced many things much before the conception of I Haven, in that this voice was of the past, but was also tied into the legacy of Hark the Herald Angel and also that of Ophlyn the Herald Angel with whom was the Father of Angel Nephi, and so I begun to realise that these circles of life unto life, were about to commence once again and to bring about the rebirth of a soul of immensity and beauty, and of peace and love, and of that of the Motherhood of Femininity and of virtue and spiritual attainment and presence.

Come my love and make haste, for the spirit has told me that we must journey to your Mother's house, yes I sense it too, then let us move as one and be guided to our destiny together, before the Heavens fall or have a change of Heart to move against us, but why do you say such a thing Anahita, I do not know, except that I feel your Heart penetrate through me, are we not of one union Nephi, Yes we are Anahita but I am still aware that the World is a troubled place and still very much open to the dictates and the trials of Man, yes I suppose if they were to witness you now as you are Risen, then maybe it is wise for you to move as they do, come let us go to see and be with Kali Ma, but tell what is she like Nephi and will she greet me and welcome me as my own Mother and Father have also greeted you.

My Mother Kali Ma, but how can I find the words to speak of such things to you, when I can hardly find the words to describe and explain the bond and the connection between us, except to say that she is many things and all things at once, she is Virtue and she is Promise, she is a Goddess and yet she is Human, she is a Woman and yet she is the Substance of the Spiritual Earth, as such are you also Anahita, is she beautiful Nephi, Beautiful, well yes, her beauty is a nurturing sanctuary of inner peace, her beauty is her love and wisdom, her beauty is her patience and understanding, her beauty is her selflessness, then I must attain and inspire to be and to like she is do you not think Nephi, well yes Anahita there are many attributes that you can aspire to learn from my Mother, but I think she would prefer it, if you were just natural self, as I believe that your calling and my Mother's calling however similar are not entirely the same thing, as my Mother was not so free to express her love and affection in such a way as you do, but freedom what is it Nephi, freedom I do not know how to say it, except that Man may believe that freedom is death, but why death Nephi, why death, are you not my freedom Nephi, yes Anahita I am your freedom and you are my beloved, well then do not speak or mention things of a deathly nature when I am so enraptured and bound up with you, I only speak of Man and nothing more Anahita only Man.

For when we returned to the World it was as if we two lovers
concealed the secrets of the universe encloaked in our being, in
that she was the Earth Mother and I was simply the Angel and the
Consort of her companionship, but as our outwardly appearance was
only merely that of a Woman and Man, then how could the World
possible know or see or think anything more about our appearance,
for we had ventured out of Africa and were by now set upon on a
course to explore the frequent and popular places where Mankind
would also frequent and gather, as Anahita had not been so far from
home, and as of yet I had also not fully engaged with the World at
large, but as we were to return to the Land of the Americas, then
at least it would be better for us to see and experience life as it was
before returning to the Home and House of that of myself and my
Mother Kali Ma.

But as for Anahita, each new place and each new sight of discovery
and scenery was something precious to behold, and yet even in the
mundane aspects of our journeying did she seem to find many more
things of interest and fascination and surprise, and yet I was always
and only concerned of her welfare and wellbeing, as if for some
unknown reason to me, that my presence was not only to abide and
journey along with her as a mere lover and companion, but also
in becoming one with whom she could rely on that would have to
watch over and protect her at all cost, for I now knew that she could
so easily become lost and distracted to the wide open spaces and
subjected influences of the all and the everything that she would
inevitably come across and find to discover,

And yet I could not stifle or restrict her nor deny her of any such
pleasures of any and yet sometimes simple and wondrous things, for
If my love for her were to be seen and felt as her freedom, then so

it should be that we would turn to love each other unconditionally and without constraints, but how was I to manage myself and steady my heart and mind, in knowing and realising that she was as of yet untainted by the World, and yet I would come to witness and to watch her grow and flower before my very eyes, for I knew that deep down, that we could not nor would not become separated so easily, in that we would eventually and completely keep each other safe and from harms reach and away from the grasping and the clutching corruptions of the World until we had arrived to the place of my birth, in that it would become time for Anahita to be introduced and acquainted with my Mother Kali Ma, with whom I would be sure and certain that she would without question, meet and greet us upon our arrival at our homeward bound destination upon arrival.

And so it was that to be that eventually when we arrived home, that my Mother Kali Ma would appear to meet us at the door, and so it was natural of her to invite us in and for her to become acquainted with Anahita, as it was at this point of time that I felt relaxed and contented to watch and observe as they would sit and talk and eat and drink and of course my Mother would inform her and share some of her own stories and experiences of times gone by, and of the many things that she had seen and witnessed and all too often played a very intrinsic part in, as it was also pleasing for Anahita to hear and to learn of such things that took place before her time and conception, and also in realising and becoming engaged in learning more about the roles of play and the integrity and the sisterhood that tied all of the Earth Mothers together.

Until all the relative stories were told and shared, and time would eventually bring us to tire in our weariness, and my Mother was also pleased and contented and filled with delight and with happiness that Anahita had come to live and to dwell amongst us, in becoming a unified family of which I believe none of the Angels of the Empyreans had never before sustained, and so this was to be new chapter however connected and steeped in the history of this Angeldom, as I knew that this beginning was to be one that would chart a different course across the spectrum of our creation, however much that I would still be conscientiously thinking out of terms of what may become and what will be within our future and within my time spell as Angel Nephi.

As the force in me I felt in my being was the force and the thought of as becoming an Angel without roots in Heaven and without regard or loyalty from one to the other, still I knew that if Mankind should fail in his trials and ambitions, even though once upon a time the fallen ones had whispered in his ears to Will him on towards a course towards damnation, that it would inevitable only lead to War, a War that could and would be fought most certainly not in the Heavens but here on Earth itself, as such was the technological and sophisticated advancement of Manmade progressions in technology becoming much more in favour of and geared towards leaning towards the creation of devastating weaponries of a divisive and destructive fashion, that perhaps sooner behind the closed doors of Man's endeavours to be or to become as such like a God, then who knows where it may lead him upon his journey of discovery into the unveiling of his own creation.

As for me I knew that I would have to serve and protect this one singular idea and notion that despite being half human and half Angel, that inevitably that this species of creation could not withstand in its own desire to move now ever more closer and nearer into fulfilling such an idealism, until every part of creation and humanity is no longer mindful or set upon a path of destruction, and so therefore I would hope to believe that within my powers of influence that Mankind should be blinded as I once was to the ways of an annihilistic approach of finality and behaviour towards each other, but whether I alone as a one Angel could indeed inspire such a creation to effectively look at its mortal self in comparison to one another, in realising and in seeing that we and they are all fundamentally the same in every way conceivable in the true eyes of the creator.

Or could it simply be that by setting themselves free from the hands of the creator and into the World unknown and at large, could only serve to set the complexities of Man so far away from the simplicities of an Angelic like nature, even though now I am resigned to the truth and the reality and the prospect of what my love for my beloved shall contend to uncover concerning this the mystery as of yet unsolved and yet still looming over the thought and the prospect of the fate of our World, as such was this mystery to be found riddled with such profound truth and consequence, that Anahita did mention it in saying to my Mother that she had a strange and yet fascinating dream, and that in the nature of this dream she had heard a voice speaking out from the depths of her soul, and so when my Mother asked and inquired if Anahita knew or had even recognised the voice, she replied in saying that she did not know it, except that the voice would know her inner most sanctum, and had given her a great feeling of wealth and emotion filled with joy and love and compassion, and that it seemed as if she knew everything about all that was as of yet not revealed or apparently so.

So was it a premonition child, no replied Anahita, then which spirit had influenced and filled you with such a blessed and overwhelming feeling, it is an Earth Mother replied Anahita, but who is it child, and what did she say or do in this dream, well she was praying I think Kali Ma, praying, praying what exactly, well I am quite sure that she was praying to God and her beloved at the same time, an Earth Mother praying, to God, but that can only mean that she is need of deliverance, well I think that she was waiting, waiting, but for what, well I think she was waiting for a miracle as I cannot explain it any other way, a miracle, but even at the best of times we all need a miracle child, but tell me, do you know the prayer she was making.

Well yes I've heard it many times before, then please share it with us Anahita, well she always says, And I will praise God in his sanctuary, And I will praise him in his mighty firmament, and I will praise him for his mighty acts, And I will praise him according to his excellent greatness! And I shall praise him with the sound of the trumpet, and I will praise him with the lute and harp! And I will praise him with stringed instruments and flutes, and I shall praise him with clashing cymbals! So let everything that breathes praise the Lord.

But tell me do you know this prayer Kali Ma, and so it was that Kali Ma did not reply or respond immediately, then eventually she turned and said I knew a Woman once, a devout Earth Mother, she was a legend and a legacy amongst us, she was also a custodian and a senior and devout figure within the household of this Matriarchal sisterhood of the Earth Mothers so true, and yet so divine and so loving and ever so peaceful, and such a beautiful soul in the way she went about her daily life, she was very much gifted, a bit like you are I suppose Anahita, well who was she, well she was the consummate Earth Mother of Hark the Herald Angel, but didn't your beloved and

Nephi's Father Ophlyn also know her, yes he did, but that was a long time ago, but what became of her.

Well my child, the truth is she died giving birth, Oh God, I am so sorry to hear that Kali Ma, no do not apologise as we Earth Mothers have our own way of dealing with these matters concerning life and death as such is the circle of life, so do you believe or think that she is ready, ready for what child, to be born again, but how can that be, because I feel and sense that she is, but you are still so young Anahita, so how can you jump to such conclusions, when you do not yet know all of our ways, yes of course I am aware that there is so much more that I can aspire to engage and learn, but I feel like I can do anything right now, anything at all, and I want too.

Well yes I suppose maybe you can, but I'm just concerned and perhaps attempting to put an old head onto such young shoulders, but tell me child are you ready for such a thing, I mean this is such powerful stuff, but Nephi and I have already consummated our love with each other, as we are now ready to begin a new chapter in our lives, as such are our destinies interlinked and intertwined not only to each other, but also along with the Earth and even the Heavens, well maybe perhaps, but is this truly you speaking Anahita and not a dream child, yes I know my own mind and own heart Kali Ma, and I am sure in my heart mind and soul that I am ready, then tell me once more, how often is it that you have felt this spiritual presence, well it seems quite natural and familiar to me, as I have felt it many times, and what did she say apart from the prayer, well she also said to complete the circle, as she has been saying that more and more ever since I met Nephi and Haven for the first time, but if it is who I think it is, then it seems that you are ready well for just about anything that life can throw at you, yes I believe that I am Kali Ma, but can please can you tell me the name of the Earth Mother.

And so it was that once again Kali Ma became silent, and then with some tears of mixed emotions that suddenly came flooding into her eyes, quietly she said, it is Selah, what Selah, yes her name is Selah, yes that's it I knew it was Sela, or Selah, or something like that, Selah yes I think it's a beautiful name and I shall be happy to complete the circle and praise God for Selah, and so with delight and surprise Kali Ma was astonished for a while at Anahita, for being so bold and proud and somewhat forthright in her pragmatism, as it was upon Anahita's immediate responses and reflection of learning and discovering which Earth Mother in particular had been awakened and revealed to her in coming forth from the spiritual realm of this World, was now being brought into the reality of all our understanding, although for a while none of us knew exactly how to react to such profoundly and yet inspiringly good and fortunate overwhelming news.

But tell me Anahita how long has it been since you and my son have become joined within this union of hearts and mind, Mother please refrain from such private questions, no my son it is very important to know, but why, because we have to be exactly sure as to when Selah might be born, Oh I see, well it has only been a few days, a few days, well yes perhaps six or seven days, very well then, as we must now ensure that if we anticipate the time ahead in that the future past has now evermore become present, then I believe that from now on it will take approximately eight months and three weeks and twenty one days and between twelve to fourteen hours before the entire cycle is complete, but how can you be so accurate, well let's just say that an Earth Mothers intuition is of paramount importance within the nature and the law of these matters in knowing exactly how these cycles effectively work and affect us

But doesn't it matter which month she is born in, of course perhaps just a little, but that is nothing to worry or be concerned about, as all we really have to do is to hope and pray that her deliverance is a peaceful and a calm and a natural one, but how can we be so sure of that, afterall will she not remember or have any memory of anything concerning her previous life, well yes but as many souls that are still somewhat dormant and asleep and must also pass through a neutralising state before their transmigration through the soul cages is complete, but pay attention and mind that these processes have nothing to do with the physical body at all, as it is only the composite aspects or the code of the internalised spirit that is to be proven, as I believe that it is there, that she will retain what is essentially and only the true and natural composition and facets of what she originally was and is uniquely herself before the physical World has allowed for any influences to make an impression or put any mark or upon her, as of when these processes of purity are fully complete well only the time spent asleep can truly say, but it can then allow for her to be born freely emancipated and unaffected by any traits or physical imprints of her previous life.

But as for the ordinary and the mundane experiences that she may have experienced or endured, will not be so apparent and will fall and break away in leaving behind was is pure spirit of non physical matter, as it is only her spirit that is to be solely engaged for this purpose and reason of definition, but what about you, I mean will she not remember you, or Hark, or Ophlyn, or her son Stefan, well yes perhaps in the mature stages of life she might recall her previous life, or have a reflection of who are the ones of whom she may have touched or affected upon her previous life at the most, but this is a matter of consequence of what her new life and role shall be over the years.

You see what you must understand Anahita is that as Earth Mothers, we must all uniquely see everything as interdependent and interconnected throughout however improbable and unlikely an event it is, as even the Earth is a living energy and entity having its own soul and spirited consciousness and composition within the ecology of creation, as it is also alive and in by being so, it is also giving and sustaining life, however remote and less apparent to the visible eye that this may be, very well then I understand Earth Mother Kali Ma, I shall stay here with you and my beloved Nephi until the baby Selah is become born again, very well then Anahita, you are most precious and welcome to stay with us as long as you see fit to dwell in this place

And so it was that with the time passing us with each and every moment, whilst taking us through each and every eventual stage of our changing state of development, as even the peaceful state of mind and soundness of being had kept pace and patience with every stride of our evolvement in seeing this Child nurturing and growing with the womb, through the realms of life, as side by side the spirit lingered in us, in bestowing its' kindnesses upon us, so as not to cause us too much trial or worry, or error and discomfort or effort as we endeared to live and to love in our commitments to one another day by day, although I knew and sensed in my heart that it troubled my Mother especially that I had less of a Will of conviction to acknowledge a God of whom I suppose could allow that those who went before me to be allowed to become fallen and to become stricken from the history of our creations revelation.

As I even knew that even Anahita's faith was also much stronger and affirmed than mine, but I am Angel, and I am created for a purpose, and I am also at the foot and the mercies of the creator in spite of what I see and witness as the truth of my reality, and yet why is it to be so, that the integrity of Man is to be so upheld and prized so highly, when in turn it would seem that we as Angels were not so privileged to the freedoms and the expressions of suchlike Men, for if we were, then we would be seen as lost or becoming wayward, and ultimately we would be classified as fallen in our actions and choices or ceasing to acknowledge ceaseless virtues, for as such was these dividing lines between Men and Angels, that they would indeed be jealous because of us, while we in turn would despise them for their freedoms, for as much as they would come to see us as being or becoming immortal in their eyes, as much as they would be free to hold us to ransom most humbly and amongst and within the dictates upon this, the terms of such an agreement of such a God of such a Kingdom.

As it was true to say that of my Mother and of my Beloved Anahita that they were both at least content and satisfied to know that the future present was becoming the present tense, and so once again I took to the skies in flight to be with those of my kind, and to see an old friend who had endured a battle which was to make of him a champion in all of our eyes, in becoming the right hand of God, but what was to take effect and transpire between us I did not know it, for if in turn it was I who were the one to have taken aim to defend the Empyreans against its foes, then at least for now I can only imagine if it would agree with me that I could have been the one to become seated and upheld within all the councils of the Heavens pertaining, then maybe this is the way that it was to be, for in my absences I had discovered the virtues of life and the promise of love within another, if for not such an ordinary Human being, then at least with an Earth Mother that loved me so.

For when I arrived at the Heavens of my creation, I did but see that all was transformed and change, and not what I had seen as before the War had broken out, but it was still a majestic and wondrous place of amazement, for the stars had all but realigned and become centered upon the Son of Angel Simeon, who was now the Herald Angel Haven, with whom I had grown accustomed too in both spirit and nature and voice of reason, although it was true to say that he was no warrior but that had somehow proven to be that he had helped and assisted and defeated his enemies by a single strike and decidedly blow, that God would be forced and caused to move against them, if not only for this place to withstand against all else.

But Haven I hath said, that you are not as you once were, nay Nephi, I too am also risen up to the point of edification of the exalted ones, and you, pray tell what of you, well let us just say that I am besides myself but content and happy appreciative of the small mercies of my simple life, nay Nephi, life and living are not at tall but simple, as they are proven to be much more than that, but pray tell me what of Anahita, Anahita, well let me say that soon she shall be with child, a child you say, yes it is true that we are one in our union, then we should fly together in the glory of her way, nay good my friend, I am not so spirited to fly in such a way, but why Nephi, why do you seem so somber my friend, as if the fate of the World weighs heavy upon you, well you see Nephi, it is but of the future of the World Haven that weighs heavily upon me, afterall is it not so that what happens on Earth also occurs in Heaven.

Nay not necessarily so Nephi, for if an Angel such as you is divided or conflicted, then it is not because of God or the Heavens, it is because the World had taken hold of your heart and influenced it in such a way, as even such Men are divided between the World that the Angel Satan has corrupted within their hearts, which has also allowed for Man's Heart and Mind to become divided, as even God hath said concerning the World in good stead of our hearts, that if we cause division, then ultimately we shall become divided from each other, but then why does this so called God not just end the World and save the righteous and be done with it, well if it were so easily to be said and done then ultimately it would be so, but I do not believe that God wants to sacrifice that which by all proportions and measures can be redeemed upon this contract and measure of covenant and agreement between the creator and the created no matter how corrupt or wayward or fallen the World may seem it is still God's creation, but then how can such a wrong be made to put right if all is so over the ages, well Nephi for us, well I believe that it is only by the graces of one as such as you and I that it can made to be put right, as this is also our salvation if we are willing and permitted to save Man from a consequence that we in turn may debate and ultimately pay for the ultimate price for in Heaven or on Earth.

As for Mans future, well this is not his destiny alone that hangs in the balance but also ours to bare also, for if Man's shadow holds all in the balance, then it is upto us to be aware that if Man were to somehow come and bring the Heavens crashing down over the Earth, then ultimately only we as the caretakers or the guardians of Man can possibly do all that we can to prevent such a calamity of insanity and madness from prevailing, as much as it is not to our advantage to remove the pillars that sustain us in order for the tree of life that is our home and habitat to be made to become uprooted, so do you not yet see the ways of God, yes Haven I see now, I see that you have put things so eloquently, but is it as true as you have shown and demonstrated, as I am also aware of the consequence and the real significance of Mans relations to us as Angels, well whether it is significant or not Nephi, the point of which I am attempting to make, is that Man is only the key, but we are the destiny are we not Haven, is it not so, well yes perhaps it is true, and yes perhaps Man is the key to everything as even unto our own undoing, of what all truth could possibly be.

Although it was written a long time ago Nephi, that once a Man said and not an Angel, that blessed is the one who does not walk in step with the wicked or stand in the way that sinners take, or sit in the company of mockers but whose delight is in the law of the Lord and who meditates on his law day and night, that person is like a tree planted by streams of water, which yields its fruit in season and who leaf does not wither Nephi, for whatever they do prospers, not so for the wicked! This is who you were Nephi, this is what you are, for God had not restricted you, or put chains about you, or held you in contempt, or denied you of anything for any reason except that you see all that is the Glory of God, as you are not bound or tied or restricted from anything such like a prisoner of conscience, do as thou heart and mind is commanded to do and all will be well in abiding forth with you Nephi.

But what about the fallen Haven, I mean why has such a judgment befallen on so many of our kind, when is it not Man that is also the true menace and an ill upon the face of the World multiplying like an infectious and unstoppable virus, nay Nephi, it is not so or such the Will of all Men, as even you have concealed it and despised it, and envied it with your own fallen spirit Nephi, yes it is true to say that they are like the chaff that one day the wind eventually blows away, therefore the wicked will not stand in the judgments nor the sinners in the assembly of the righteous, for the Lord watches over the ways of the righteous, but as for the ways of the wicked which inevitably leads to destruction, and so it is upto you to choose which path it is that is truth, and which path it is that is right, as you are free and at liberty to stand where you choose to stand, but should you choose to stand where the ground beneath your feet is not worthy, then you may become lost to all else in that which you were or wish or desire to attain and defend, for how can a tree without roots surely prosper and grow, and so here me when I say unto you Nephi, do not become befallen so as to suffer the same fate of Asmodeus and the others, for as of when may come the day that Man shall turn to curse the Sun, so shall he also be found not to be cursing the God of creation, but the bright and morning star that is also Satan

And so it was that with that thought, that before I left this newly constructed realm of the merging heavens to return to the place of my earthly home which was by now calling out to me, with the idea that I was at least by now convinced by Haven, that this newly Heralded Angel, that even in the darkest recesses of my mind where my thoughts would linger, that Heaven itself would not be against me, even if I were to think, or to choose to do otherwise, as it was as if understanding, and forgiveness and compassion had by now become something of value to me, and of something of which by now I had somehow succumb and surrender and yielded to believe in.

But tell me one thing Nephi, for if you already knew of the significance of the Bow of Nimrod, then why did you not choose to take aim and vanquish the fallen ones yourself, why, well let me tell you why Haven, it is because I know of no other Angel that would or could hold such a promising and virtuous and sincere nature other than that of you my friend, as I now see and believe that it was your destiny to bring about a significant change that we could all eventually come to love and admire, and respect and adhere too, but it could so easily have been you that would herald in such a different outcome, Nephi if you had taken charge of this matter, and what would I gain if I chose to carry out such an act and lose all else that I have now found to cherish in the beloved Anahita.

It is far better that it is you and not me now holding this position of high authority and esteem Haven, nay it would and could not have been the same outcome, don't you see, that you had already achieved such a position of grace amongst the Celestials and the Empyreans, and this Bow that you now hold and wield within your possession can only offer to serve and to confirm such a blessing of hope for all mankind and Angels alike, but as for me my friend, I shall now be gone from this place, as it is my beloved that awaits my return and to learn of the good and fortunate fate that has befallen upon you, in that now it had gifted and lifted you up to the wonders of your edification, yes I now know that what is invested in you is of a worthiness amongst any of the ranks and positions that any Angel of this realm would hope to hold onto so dearly.

And so it was that Several months had by now passed, and the time was drawing nearer and nearer, and closer and closer to the birth of our first child, and so we begun to make preparations for the newly awaited baby to come into our lives, as such was the nervous tensions and expectations of an Angelic Father in becoming, that I was often on edge as to when exactly Selah would arrive to us, and so it was to be that along with Anahita and my Mother Kali Ma by her side, that they had already taken the steps for my beloved to enter into a hospital and to be made prepared and comfortable within the Maternity Wing, as such was my emotions for the first time, that I found myself doing the one thing that I thought and felt that I would not and could not do, and that was to speak with God, as such was the intensity of the prevailing situation, that I prayed and hoped that he would listen to the least of his subjects in asking for Selah to be granted safe passage into this World.

And so as I gathered my thoughts and my wits about me, as the day and the expected moment had finally come, and Anahita who was by now already experiencing regular contractions and was by now ready to give birth, and so as it was that with a few nurses in attendance and Kali Ma by her side giving her support and willing and urging her to take deep breaths and to push and to breathe and to push and to breathe, until eventually I could see the crown of the baby's head appear, and so now it was with great hope and excitement and elation, that soon after several more repetitions of pushing and heavy gasping and breathing, that in all her efforts, Selah was now delivered to us, as such was the beauty and the awe and the wonder of seeing this act of life come into being, that now I finally knew and accepted, that if there was a God, then perhaps he had heard me from deep within the depths of my calling out to him from such a lowly place.

Come darling Nephi, for this is your beloved daughter and child, the Earth Mother Selah, place your hands upon her, and hold her, and bless her with the Aura of the Angel that you are, and love her, and adore her, for she is come to us in our time of need, in knowing that God has not abandoned us, and that she has fulfilled and satisfied all that is good about this World, and that she has blessed us once again with her presence in coming forth to be with us to remove our woes and to satisfy and complete our union of happiness, and so it was that in my heart and mind, I finally now knew and felt that in the presence of Selah my beautiful daughter, that my life and union with the Earth Mother Anahita had somehow transformed everything in me in an instant, as all around and about me was seemingly so, and so it was to be that the circle was complete and so too was the emerging Heavens above the Earth also complete, in that a blessing had once again come forth to shine a light upon us all and to show us the way.

ᚪuthors Notes

The Angel Babies Story for me, was very much written and inspired by many feelings of expression, that was buried very deeply inside of me, as it was through my own exchanges, and relationships, and journeying, and upon the discovery of both negative and positive experiences, that often challenged my own beliefs, and personal expectations of what I thought or felt was my own life's purpose, and reason for being and doing, and very much what any one of us would expect to be the result, or the outcome of their own personal life choices based upon the status quo of our own design or choosing.

The story within itself, very much maintains its own conception of intercession from one person to another, as we can only contain the comprehension of the things that we most relate too, and that which most commonly resembles and reflect our own emotions and experiences, by tying in with something tangible that either connects, or resonate at will deeply within us, as many of us have the ability and intuit nature, to grasp things not merely as they are presented to us, but how things can also unfold and manifest in us, that are sometimes far beyond our everyday imaginings, and that are also equally hard to grasp and somewhat difficult to comprehend and let alone explain.

As we often learn to see such challenges and difficulties as these, especially in young minds, that react in responsive ways and are also equally gifted, or equally find it in themselves in life changing circumstances, to deal with prevailing situations, that most of us would take for granted, and would naturally see as the average norm, as we are all somewhat uniquely adjusted to deal with the same prevailing situation very differently, or even more so to uniquely perceive it in very different ways.

As for the question of how we all independently learn to communicate through these various means of creative, or artistic, or spiritual measures, is also simply a way of communicating to God as in prayer, as well as with one another, as all aspects are one of the same creation, as to whether such forms of expression can personify, or act as an intermediate medium, or channel to God, or indeed from one person to another, is again very much dependent upon the nature of its composition and expression, and the root from which it extends, and so for us to believe that our forbearers, or indeed our ancestors have the ability to intercede for us in such spiritual terms upon this our journey through life, is very much to say, that it is through their life's experiences, that we have become equipped, and given a wealth, and a portion of their life's history, with which for us to make our own individual efforts and choices, for us to be sure and certain of the way, in which we shall eventually come to be.

When we take a leap of faith, it is often into the unknown, and it is often associated with, or stems from the result of our constant fate being applied and presented to us in the context of a fear or phobia, insomuch so, that we must somehow, or at least come face to face with, or deal with, or come to terms with these matters arising, that are usually our own personal concerns, or worries, or anxieties toward a balanced or foreseeable reality, which is often beyond our immediate control, in that we are attempting to define and deal with this systematic physical, and spiritual progression, in the hope and the faith that we can resolve these personal matters, so as to allow us to put the mind and the heart at ease and to rest.

As it is often through our rationalizing, and our affirmation, and our professing or living with our beliefs, that what we often call, or come to terms with through our acceptance, is that through faith, belief and worship in God, that such personal matters, can easily be addressed, and dealt with, so as to overcome when facing such difficult and challenging obstacles, as even when in response to a negative impact that can have a harmful effect upon our physical bodies and being, we also often rely upon this same faith in the physical terms of our living and well being to guide us, and especially where we are often engaged in rationalizing with this phenomena, in the context of our faith, hope and belief, which often requires and demands us to look upon the world in a completely different way, so that we can reach far beyond the rational expectations of our own reality, and perceive to look forward into that of our metaphysical world.

As it is through this metaphysical world of all irrationality, and chaos and confusion, that a leap of faith is required to pass through and beyond the unknown context of our rational and conscious reality, and thus so as far as we can see, to understand our consciousness, as we believe it should be, in that we are contained in every aspect of our faith, hope and belief, as we are often presented with more than just a rational imagination, of what lies beyond our eventful fate or worries and concerns, and so within the mind of dreams, we are presented with a super imagination, where extraordinary things exist and take effect much beyond our physical comprehension, although very much aligned to the interconnectedness within our emotions, that brings with it a super reality, where we can accept the tangibility of these dreams upon realizing them, so as to be found and understood, as when we are found to be waking up in our day to day reality and activity, but also in choosing not to deny or extinguish these dreams as mere dreams, but to accept, and to see them, or refer to them as signs.

As of when we see such tell tale signs, or such premonitions forgoing, or foreboding us in our fate, it is very much that these signs often impact the most upon that of our conscious minds, as they are very much presented to us in an informative and abstract way, very much like a picture puzzle that we are busily attempting to piece together and work out, and very much in the way that we are attempting to put the heart and the mind at ease and to rest, so as to secure peace of mind in order to find and establish and maintain inner peace, as such signs as these, are often the ones that I am referring too, and can often and easily be presented to us in many ways, but to be sure and certain, if they are Godly or Divining messages upon intuition and translation, very much depends and largely relies upon us as individuals, as to what we are naturally engaged in and pursuing, in the same hope and light of the context, of this experience of such a Godly nature.

As such experiences are crucial and key, as to how we deal with any or all relationships, especially when we are developing a relationship within the Godly aspects of our lives, as more often than not, when we use such phrases and metaphors as, 'Going through a Door' or 'Crossing a Bridge, it is simply by saying such statements as these, or putting things in this way or context, that we decidedly know and acknowledge that a big change is about to occur, and develop or happen to us, and so we in ourselves are becoming equipped and prepared to deal with such changes, as they shall determine what shall be the eventual outcome of our fate, as there may already have been so many foretelling signs, much before the final impact or infinite sign is presented to us, insomuch so, that it may have already been subtly presented to us, much before the true perspective or picture of our reality has come to fruition and presented to us as a whole.

The whole being, is that which pieces itself together, with all the necessary facets and aspects of our Human Nature, Personality, Mannerisms and Characteristics and Traits, as all in all, it presents to us a vision, which sets us apart from one another, but also equally ties us all together in the event and act of completing our picture and journey through life, and it is through these instincts that we all naturally possess, and is all that is inextricably woven into the metaphysical fabric and the spiritual aspects of the heart and mind, and of those that are channeled along the lines of the minds meridians, and the intricate channels that give way to apprehensible intuitive mental awareness of signs and dreams, and or premonitions or visions, of how, or what we may choose to accept, or to objectively analyze, or to take note of and perceive in communication, or indeed how God may choose to communicate with or through us.

As it is in our realizing that within our personal fate and decisiveness, that we are calling upon, and facing a reality, that questions and presents itself to us all, as something that is profoundly spiritual and ambiguous, in relation to what we are all intrinsically held and bound by within our faith and beliefs, in that what we expect is about to unravel itself before us, as we begin to discover all that in which we are, as such is the expectation and the realization in our phobias and fears, that we may begin to readdress or even regress, or desist in such a course of action concerning these doubts and deliberations, so as not to offset or to promote any ideas that may bring about any personal demise, or disharmony, or disunity, that may trigger any negative aspectual forecasts or emotions within ourselves, as it is such a self fulfilling reality, that we are all in subjection too, in creating along and upon our own individual paths of merits and natural progression, that naturally such phenomena is presented and revealed to us as a whole, and is often profoundly real and yet maintains its simplicity, and is quite ordinarily so upon our realization of it, as if by mere chance that somehow deep down we already knew, that when we became aware of it, we somehow knew it to be so.

As it is these lessons in life, that are to be learnt from such self affirming challenges, so as to test our minds imagination and of course that which is at the very heart, of how we in our Human nature, can so easily push our abilities far beyond the boundaries, upon the premise of what is, or what is not possible, which brings to mind the verse and saying of the scripture and that is to say, that if anyone adds or takes away from this book, then so too shall their part be added or taken away, and yet if we continue further along this point, it also goes on to ask, who is worthy to remove this seal, so as to reveal the dream or the foreknowledge that we may all come to terms with our natural agreement and acceptance of it, as it is in knowing and accepting what shall befall us in our fate, as to what choice of action we must or can take, as such are the phobias and fears of trepidation that also gives way to the rise of hope, so that we may come face to face with destiny.

As with each new day comes a new beginning, and with each new beginning comes new hopes and new expectations, as there are also new obstacles and challenges to overcome, as such is the dawning of life, to present to us all, such necessary and redeemable qualities within the observations of our lives, for to have hope, is to look up toward the heavens, and to quietly and silently know, that within this observation, that the sky or indeed the heavens, are still upheld by the forces of nature, that govern from above albeit much to our amazement and expectations, and that life is ordinarily and justly so, as we in our appreciation cannot always see beyond that which is so perfectly bound and set in motion with us in this universe, as we simply learn to believe and accept that this is the way of our living and all things besides us, as we are within all that has become created and laid out before us.

And yet with this new day dawning, if not for us to simply wake up and to use our hopes, and our aspirations to ascend beyond the obvious point of creation, and to apply our spiritual nature and positive will of motivation toward it, and it toward us upon reflection, as in our overcoming and prevailing, within its and our own destiny and deliverance, as such is also our descent to take warmth and courage, and comfort and refuge, when we lay down to take rest and sleep beneath the Moon and the Stars above, is also to take strength and peace of mind, in the hope and the understanding that a new day beginning, and a new dawning shall be presented to us once again, as this is the way of the life that we have come to know it, within our own divine ability and acceptance of it.

As much as life is and can very much be a challenge, it also appears to state, that there is a thread of universal commonality running through the whole of creation no matter what we profess to live and abide by as human beings, as for me the basis of these requirements that extend from this commonality is food, shelter, clothing, companionship, and a sense of connection or clarity derived from self awareness, that is not to say that there is not much more for broad scope beyond this basic measure and requirement that puts us all on an equal footing with one another, no matter where we inhabit or dwell in the world.

And so what and where are we permitted upon this universal basis, to gravitate towards, or indeed to excel to, in order to fulfill our existential experiences and engage with our full potential, as many of us in our progression towards modernity, would indeed interpretate this kind of idea or philosophy, depending upon which part of the world we lived in or inhabited, as being very much viewed differently realized upon that same broad basis, which also brings me to ask, and to question, and to examine this brave new world within this context, or indeed as some would profess to say or mention, within this new world order, or new world system, as there is much to address and to consider for all concerned.

For once we have evolved and grown and matured away from our basic needs and requirements, it would also appear that many of us who have indeed excelled, or concluded in the context of a post-modernistic era of environment or society, to have almost achieved something, which is of a value, or at least on a par with something that is equally attributed, to that of a spiritual level of attainment, or indeed enlightenment, but when we address the cost of such achievement, we also begin to see that we are still somewhat grounded in our best efforts by this basic requirement, which is to achieve, acquire, and survive at will, and to endure, and to live, and to abide by such new discoveries of achievements.

As even in this progress and achievement of what we would wish, or presume to call a new world, how do we fairly address or balance, or differentiate between those of us who are yet to grasp the basis of this understanding that is required for us to excel, or indeed for

Clive Alando Taylor

us to fly, or indeed to reach the highest spiritual level of attainment of understanding, of being, doing, and knowing, as in realizing that indeed not many of us could have, or would have had the opportunity, or indeed the privilege, of exercising such expressions of freedom in our new found world.

As some of us are fundamentally held by the very conventions of what is required upon this, a basic level of our independence, maintenance, and survival, to regulate and maintain the simplicity of ourselves, and yet once we have experienced and entertained this new idea inside such a concept, our first response is how should we, or what should we do in order to engage with one another, to bring about its universality as a basic principle and as a must for all concerned, and how can it be any good for us, if indeed we all profoundly have separate agendas, or different ideals, as to what should, or could take precedence over the basic and fundamental needs to live out our lives, when food, and shelter, and clothing, and companionship, and a sense of self, or a clarity of awareness is needed at the very heart of what it is, to not only be, but remain humane.

As for the background, or indeed the backdrop, and the combining and dedicated efforts, that it has taken me as a writer to come to arrive at within this story of the Angel Babies, and of course the time that it has taken for me, to construct, and to collate the necessary, and if I may say worthy and worthwhile aspects, for this particular body of work to become written and completed within the trilogy of the Angel Babies, I would very much like just like to inform the readership, that upon exploration and construction of this body of work, that I myself as a person, have experienced several variables of conversions upon my spiritual and emotional being, upon the instruction and initiation of bringing the series of these books into the light.

For had I not been introduced into the many schools of thought and allied faiths of Christianity, Islam, Hare Krsna, Hindu, Buddhism, Dao and Shinto, that it may never have transpired or surmounted, or indeed would have been very much an arduous and challenging task, to find the right motivation for the narrative, very much needed and applied, with which to find and devise the relative inspiration, and ideas explored and written within the context and narrative of the characters and the storyline that I have presented to you as an author.

About the Author

Clive Alando Taylor was born on the 14th February 1969
In South West London and is the youngest son of Six siblings Keith, Nadine, Leroy, Danny ad Neville, born to Joel Ezekiel Taylor & Isolyn Icilda Taylor. As the youngest child of five, Clive has always maintained a positive outlook on life through his faith, studies and interests In World Religions, Humanity and Philosophy, Music, Dance and Poetry, although Clive's upbringing was initially nurtured in the Pentecostal Church Clive has also spent several years of his life studying Islam, Buddhism and Taoism and other minor based faiths of religious and philosophical teachings as it has been through this calling and aspiration for life that has allowed him to challenge such ideas as Race, Colour, and Gender.

As both a writer and musician of music and literature Clive has always explored the ideas and themes relating to the Human condition and Human experience, in both, Love, Life and Spirituality, as an coming from a faith based artistic background, Clive has always maintained a very pious and humble background but has always challenged himself to seek beyond the veil of Life and into Life's mysteries, as it is through the perceptibility of this matter that Clive has always through his imagination and literary writings manage to capture at the very core of this exploratory medium, the very essence of both a poetic and compassionate nature within his work, that Clive has spent much of my time thinking of suitable names for things which had often crept and arisen out of the subconscious matter of his psyche, or at least animate names or titles for of Songs and Poems and even Short or Extended Narratives, that had led his enduring imaginative experience which at least summoned, or brought forth and yielded and lent itself to the light of his life.

Even though Clive was completely aware and awake in experiencing this causality and happening of his experience which was often put much beyond his physical and practical control, although equally aware of the transition, he did not know the root, or the true depth of reason, or the inner reason why, or the outer reason of wherefore, that this external and now internalized experience were somehow to be found to be dawning upon, or happening upon his nature, As Clive often felt that as time wore on, that he was continuously changing and becoming, or realizing that he was becoming attached to a part of something of that which was too farfetched for him if not solitarily in his existential reasoning to fathom both commonly and logically, as if the feeling of dying had somehow transported and led to the exhilarant feeling of living, as also as if these the names of animate life forms and ideas, or as to, or whether they existed or not, if only upon the plains of spiritual consciousness or dreams or not.

As Clive did only serve to notice that in observing and noting and knowing, or at least truly and sincerely understanding, if only to appreciate and realize to relate to the experience, but it was almost certain that it was significant enough to Clive that in a sort of so many strange ways, albeit through obscurity, that he had somehow allowed himself, or to at least be a host, or a vessel and a channel for which in many unexplainable ways, to be overcome by this inquiring and inspiring, if not appealing force, of by which in doing so I did surrender to it.

As a writer and a poet and as an artist and performer, I have always felt the need to convey my thoughts through the artistic expression of words and music and even through the unspoken medium of movement and motion, as much as it is up to the creativity of a writer which is for me to capture or to record these moments as they unfold and take shape revealing their naked truths in the purest of forms of their suggestions and clues towards a revelation unknowingly becoming attuned and responsive to the reciprocal mind, as I have come to learn and engage in the process that the language and the words, also each independently have their own hidden inner depth when spoken, or as when heard or as when read, as each processed word proceeds one after the other, building a foundation, creating layer upon layer until their volume is felt.

Whether I choose to promote this idea upon a line of questioning, or examining, or analyzing, a stand of truth by capturing a piece of reality, or whether I am entranced by the enchantment of something more sublime like a mystery, or a fantasy, is even somewhat inspirational to me as to how my thoughts of expression and energy are channeled through such a medium and a basic quality in challenging my ability to write paragraph after paragraph and page after page, until ordinarily the mundane of perfection of the subjective object is met and begins to excite me, as writing is also very much an internal journey towards understanding the inner self and examination of the reflective world that surrounds us all, insomuch that we are constantly redefining and readjusting to all that is apparently so and open to see.

As to whether we can learn to accept through interpretation of all that is extended before us, is also to glance in a mirror and to attempt to recognize if all is as it appears to be, As I also find that being a writer also has its' holistic and therapeutic benefits in exploring and exercising one's ability to understand and to comprehend the subject matter that is at hand, arising out of the consciousness, a bit like a jigsaw puzzle in need of being pieced and placed together in order to create and make sense out of theoretical chaos as such is the genie of out of the bottle in becoming a writer.

As a young boy at school, I always found myself playing with words & rhymes especially when it came to writing poetry, it wasn't the fact that I was especially gifted or talented, but it was mainly my enthusiasm, and style & ability to be creative with words and rhyme in my own unique way, although in this day and age some may regard this as a small degree of autism but I'm not quite certain about that, as many of my peers could be just as challenging and inventive about writing prose creatively. When I left school at the age of 16 I attended dance school and was as far removed from literature as anyone could be, but I always kept a diary and also decided to study English Language part time.

During break time and in between classes once again I would find myself writing & exploring various themes using rap, rhyme and spoken word to amuse myself and my fellow classmates. At that time I didn't take it too seriously, but I loved the fact that through expression coupled with the effect of creative writing was becoming an inspiration to me as well as a positive tool for expression.

During my early adulthood I went through a depression which resulted in a nervous breakdown and I was admitted into hospital for several months and was later diagnosed as suffering from chronic schizophrenia, which is something that I have had to accept and live with up until now, although my life had changed dramatically from being a potential dancer and performance artist, I was now being made to be aware of a new and changing world, that I would now have to accept as my reality, so along with my diagnosis and the stigma that I would have to endure, I decided to lean more towards spirituality, which allowed my point of view on life to change toward a more positive outlook on life, whilst allowing me the choice and direction to move on the best way that I could.

For a while I also studied other academic subjects like psychology and social policy, but I was still very much drawn to the world of performing arts, especially dance and music, and so during my early 30's I returned back to studying movement theory and music in an attempt to regain something more in tune with my original path and career choice, although by now I felt it was a little too late to achieve my intended goal and dream in the world of performing arts.

Over time I realized that I had written and explored many themes through my experiences, from songs to poems and from the odd script to a storyline that had captured my minds imagination or psyche, and so of lately I have pursued this level of equilibrium and understanding with vigor, but not only to help myself but to help others to come to terms with and to understand the world in which we all live and how we contribute too it, having mentioned all this I am not so sure or certain if this qualifies me to be a writer or validates my work or my ideas in literature or literary terms, but I have learnt to accept my life through these working ideas and challenges as either a constant and perpetual cycle which I have tried to capture through my writing.

If I were to describe any traits or attributes about myself, albeit good or bad, or otherwise, then I would best describe myself as being spontaneous, communicative, unorthodox, innovative and revolutionary within my approach and attitude to most if not all things pertaining or arising out of all matters of consciousness, as I would also choose to add to the face that I am quite original in possessing a somewhat detached mind upon its application to most circumstances presenting itself to me, as I am also quite fairly democratic and eccentric in part and pleasure, although very much the humanitarian and philanthropic and sincerely diplomatic in my advances of any exceptional and natural expectations.

Sociably I am tolerant, altruistic, progressive in my literary application of ideas, and so as to indicate my preferences, my favorite colours are white, pale yellow, green, and electric blue, although outwardly I can be found to be a little uncompromising, and unconventional, and a natural rebel with a curious and cold practicality of eccentric instability, as I see the future and all things transpiring, with both a noble and soulful and spiritual distinctive clarity, as a writer and a poet, and as an artist and performer, I have always felt the need to convey my thoughts through the artistic expression of words and music, and even through the unspoken medium of movement and motion, as much as it is up to the creativity of a writer, which is for me to capture, or to record these moments as they unfold and take shape revealing their naked truths in the purest of forms of their suggestions and clues towards a revelation unknowingly becoming attuned and responsive to the reciprocal mind.

As naturally overtime I have come to learn and to engage in the process that the language and the words, also along with which each independently have their own hidden inner depth when pronounced and spoken, or as when heard, or as when read when written, as each processed word proceeds one after the other, building a foundation, creating layer upon layer, until their volume is felt, whether I choose to promote this idea upon a line of questioning, or examining, or analyzing, a stand of truth by capturing a piece of reality, or whether I am entranced by the enchantment of something more sublime, like a mystery, or a fantasy, which is also even somewhat of an inspiration to me, as to how my thoughts of expression and energy are channeled through such a medium and a basic quality in challenging my ability to write paragraph after paragraph and page after page, until ordinarily the mundane efforts of perfection of the subjective object is met with and then begins to excite me.

As writing is also very much an internal journey towards understanding the inner self and examination of the reflective world that surrounds us all, insomuch that we are constantly redefining and readjusting to all that is apparently so and open to see, but as to whether we can learn to accept that through the interpretation of all that is extended before us, is also to glance in a mirror and to attempt to recognize if all is as it appears to be, as I also find that being a writer also has its' holistic and therapeutic benefits in exploring and exercising one's ability to understand and to comprehend the subject matter that is at hand, and found to be arising out of the consciousness, a bit like a jigsaw puzzle in need of being pieced and placed together in order to create and make sense out of theoretical chaos, as such is the genie that is out of the bottle for me in both being and becoming a writer.

~ Clive Alando Taylor

REFERENCE

Empyrean - (Heaven/Angelic Dwelling Place)
Haven - (Hope)
Hark the Herald - (The Listening Angel)
Angel Nephi - (Nephilim)
Simeon - (The Protecting Angel)
Stefan - (The Angel Of Love)
Ophlyn - (The Fallen Angel)
Papiosa - Father Of Anahita / Character Depicting Good and Evil)
Leoine - Mother Of Anahita / (Bastion & Sentient)
**Men Shen - (Taoist Interpretation meaning
/ Guardians of the Door)**
Angel Of Justice - (figuratively)
Anahita - (Earth Mother)
Selah - (Earth Mother)
Kali Ma - (Hindu Supreme Goddess or Black Earth Mother)
Gabriel - (Archangel)
Michael - (Archangel)
Raguel - (Archangel)
Raphael - (Archangel)
Remiel - (Archangel)
Uriel - (Archangel)
Zerachiel - (Archangel)
Nejeru - (New Jerusalem)
Golden Dawn - (The Future)
Throne Of God - (Emerald Green/Ophanim)

Infinitive
Angelus Domini
A Tao.House Product /Angel Babies Realm VI
INSPIRIT*ASPIRE*ESPRIT*INSPIRE

Valentine Fountain of Love Ministry

Info contact: **tao.house@live.co.uk**

Copyright: Clive Alando Taylor 2015